MYTHIC

A QUARTERLY SCIENCE FICTION & FANTASY MAGAZINE

ISSUE #1 | WINTER 2016

TABLE OF CONTENTS

MYTHIC
A Quarterly Science Fiction & Fantasy Magazine
ISSUE # 1 WINTER 2016

Published by Founders House Publishing LLC

MYTHIC: A Quarterly Science Fiction & Fantasy Magazine
is a project and publication of Founders House Publishing LLC.

www.mythicmag.com

www.foundershousepublishing.com

ISBN 13: 978-1-945810-01-5
ISBN 10: 1-945810-01-7

Printed in the United States of America

MYTHIC is quarterly magazine published by Founders House Publishing LLC. We publish speculative fiction, specifically science fiction and fantasy. Our mission is to expand the range of what is currently possible within both genres. We like new perspectives and new spins on familiar tropes. Diversity is a hallmark of our vision.

One year, four-issue subscriptions to *MYTHIC* cost *$40*. You can subscribe by visiting www.mythicmag.com or make out checks to Founders House Publishing and send them to the following address: 614 Wayne Street, Suite 200A / Danville, IL 61832

If you are interested in submitting to *MYTHIC*, you can visit our website for information regarding our submission guidelines.

www.mythicmag.com/submissions.html

EDITOR IN CHIEF

SHAUN KILGORE

DESIGN & LAYOUT

SHAUN KILGORE

SPECIAL THANKS TO

JOHN MICHAEL GREER

SPECIAL THANKS TO OUR FOUNDATION SUBSCRIBERS

ANDRO HSU
ROBERT WALSHE
DEREK KEELE
TIMOTHY WHITMORE-WOLF
JAMES GEMMILL
JOAN HOWE
THOMAS WILLIAMS
CATHERINE TROUTH
DYLAN SIEBERT
TREVOR HANDLEY
E.J. SHUMAK
JEFF HARRISON
DONALD MCDONNELL
GLENDA WEST
GREG BAKA
DANIEL BARBOUR
JEFFERY VONDY
WILLIAM MICHIE
JAMES JENSEN
DANIEL NAJIB

Coming Next Issue in *MYTHIC*

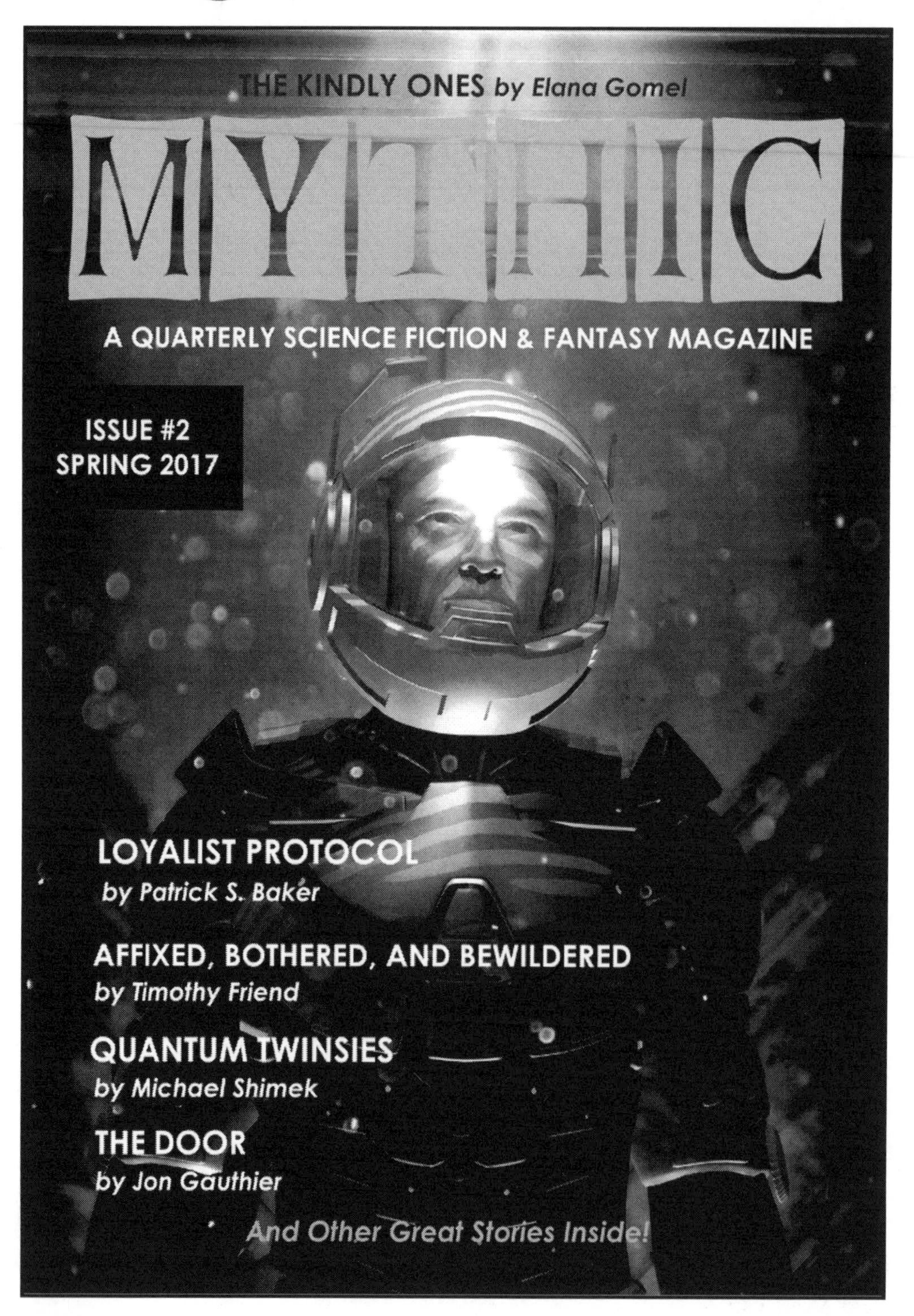

CONTRIBUTORS

Kirsten Cross lives in a cottage on Exmoor complete with roses around the door and a six-mile round trip to the nearest village. She spends her days writing web content and her evenings and weekends getting up to all sorts of shenanigans, including surfing, martial arts, rebuilding old army motorcycles and wild swimming. She's a regular contributor to the acclaimed SNAFU military horror series, and has also made forays into Steampunk and Science Fiction. She's currently writing her first full-length novel. She's also, for some unknown reason, surprisingly good at welding.

Catherine McGuire has three decades of published poetry and two children's sci-fi novels published by TSR. She has four poetry chapbooks and a full-length poetry book, *Elegy for the 21st Century* (FutureCycle Press). Her novel *Lifeline* will be published soon by Founders House Publishing.

Find her at www.cathymcguire.com.

Jean Graham's short fiction has appeared in the anthologies *Time of the Vampires, Misunderstood, Dying to Live,* and *Memento Mori,* among others. She lives in San Diego, CA, with 5000 books, six cats, and one husband. Visit her website at http://jeangraham.20m.com.

D. A. D'Amico is a playful soul trapped in the body of a grumpy old man. In early years, this presented a problem, but the author's grown into the role quite nicely. He's had more than forty works published in the last few years in venues such as Daily Science Fiction, Crossed Genres, and Shock Totem…among others. He's also begun transcribing his memoirs onto the moon with a 25 petawatt pulse laser borrowed from his evil twin, but he's afraid the beautiful 12-point Old Century Gothic font he chose is lost among the bright dust of Tycho crater. He can be found at http://www.dadamico.com, or on Facebook at authordadamico, or in the crevices between those pesky floorboards you've been meaning to fix—if you can find him.

Joanna Michal Hoyt lives with her family on a Catholic Worker farm in upstate NY where she spends her days tending goats, gardens and guests and her evenings reading and writing odd stories. Her fiction has appeared in publications including Crossed Genres, Daily Science Fiction, and the

Mysterion anthology of Christian speculative fiction.

Ramon Rozas III lives in West Virginia, where he writes speculative fiction. When not writing, Ramon practices law. You can follow him on twitter (@ramonrozas) or at his blog, www.ramonrozasiii.blogspot.com

Timothy Rock resides in central Pennsylvania where he's chasing a bachelor's degree. When he isn't working at the bar or studying for law school, he writes, and hopes one day to make something of it.

John Michael Greer is the author of more than forty nonfiction books and four novels, most recently *The Weird of Hali: Innsmouth*, the first volume of a Lovecraftian epic fantasy series. He lives in a red brick mill town in the north central Appalachians with his wife Sara.

David Senti is a part-time writer and father of three with an intense interest in history, Scholastic philosophy and the principles of governance. He is a devout Catholic and hopes to publish his first novel soon. He is married to Jody Senti, who is just super. Beyond that, he is thoroughly uninteresting.

D.B. Keele, a former library professional and occasional writer and editor, graduated from Indiana University with a B.A. in English. He lives in central Indiana. You can follow him on Twitter @DerekBKeele.

Shaun Kilgore is the author of various works of fantasy, science fiction, and a number of nonfiction works. He has also published numerous short stories and collection. His books appear in both print and ebook editions. Shaun is the publisher and editor of MYTHIC: A Quarterly Science Fiction & Fantasy Magazine. He lives in eastern Illinois. Visit www.shaunkilgore.com for more information.

Frank Kaminski is an ardent Seattle-area peak oiler, a connoisseur of deindustrial fiction and a longtime book reviewer for Resilence.org and Mudcitypress.com. He's been happily car-free for the past 10 years.

A QUICK SHOUT OUT AND SPECIAL THANKS TO OUR PATRONS ON *PATREON*.

YOU'RE HELPING US MAY MYTHIC BETTER ONE ISSUE AT A TIME.
www.patreon/mythicmag

INTRODUCTION
DREAMS COME TRUE

BY SHAUN KILGORE

Welcome, everyone! I'm delighted to present the very first issue of **MYTHIC: A Quarterly Science Fiction and Fantasy Magazine.** I have to say that this moment has been a long time in the making for me. I've always wanted my own magazine and now I'm finally at a point where I can produce one the way I'd always imagined it.

I spent years tinkering with magazines, writing and drawing them in my youth, eventually stapling them together and nearly launching one that included content by me and a bunch of my friends. Those first efforts were crude but filled with promise.

I couldn't abandon the notion of producing a publication. In time, I became a book publisher and the idea of a magazine was right there waiting for its time. I published anthologies via Founders House Publishing, my company, with the help of author John Michael Greer, who edited the *After Oil* series of SF anthologies (reviews of which are included in this issue) and generously wrote both an essay and a story for the first issue.

Magazines are not easy things to create. There's a lot of work both editorially and in terms of interior and exterior design to produce a look and a style that works well and offers the reader a good experience. I've been studying its form and I'm always learning.

So, here I am at the editorial helm of a brand new publication dedicated to publishing stories of wonder and imagination. Science fiction and fantasy have always been prominent in my reading (and writing) choices so it made sense to step back into those waters when it came to publishing short fiction.

My interests are much broader than in the past so that has carried over into the sort of decisions I will be making as an editor. As some of you may now, the genres often get pigeon-holed and perhaps they've both fallen into ruts over time. The aim of MYTHIC is to provide a venue where other visions of science fiction and fantasy may again flourish as they once did in the pulp publications of the early to mid 20th century.

While, there is much focus on the hard type of science fiction, I'm not necessarily interested in those stories primarily. It doesn't have to be scientifically feasible to be sci-fi. By the same token, it doesn't have to be all about space travel or take place in futures laden with high tech. There are other futures to be explored and certainly there's more to science than technological progress.

Similarly, with fantasy, you often get people thinking about the genre in shorthand like anything with stock characters like dragons, elves, dwarves in them or taking place in some version of Medieval Europe or with the urban variety, supernatural beings like vampires, werewolves, etc. Naturally, the genre is much broader than this narrow vision. Any avid reader of fantasy knows this. But, with this, I want to see stories that dig deeper, incorporate different cultural traditions, and strive for diversity in terms of characters and approaches.

This does not mean I don't want stories that fit traditional ideas. I like those kinds of stories too. I'm sure those reading MYTHIC agree.

So with my needs as an editor out in the open for writers, I hope you, dear reader, will enjoy the selection of stories I've put together for this inaugural issue.

Thanks for your interest in MYTHIC. There will be plenty of great fiction in the coming issues. I hope you'll follow along as we strive to improve the quality of this magazine with every issue.

Interested in submitting stories to MYTHIC? We prefer electronic submissions. You may email us at the following address:

submissions@mythicmag.com

We do accept paper submissions. You can send them to the following address:

Shaun Kilgore
MYTHIC Submissions
420 Commercial Street
Danville, IL 61832

For more complete submission guidelines and any other information you may visit our website:

www.mythicmag.com

THE NEXT GOLDEN AGE

AN ESSAY ON SCIENCE FICTION AND FANTASY

BY JOHN MICHAEL GREER

Every branch of literature has its flood tides and ebb tides, its eras of expansion and its periods of retrenchment, and science fiction and fantasy are no exception. Glance back over the history of both genres, and it's easy enough to tell the decades when new ground was being broken and the audience swelled, from those in which the writers by and large settled into comfortable ruts and the readers, those who were left, could mostly be found in an assortment of fan subcultures. Compare the golden age of pulp science fiction and fantasy in the 1920s and 1930s with the leaner period of the 1940s and 1950s, or the rapid growth and radical experimentalism of paperback SF and fantasy from the 1960s through the mid-1980s with the contracting markets and increasingly stereotyped subgenres that followed, and the systole and diastole of the collective imagination takes little effort to spot.

One of the things that makes this rhythm intriguing is that much of it was shaped by the emergence and maturation of new forms of publishing. What made the golden age of the 1920s and 1930s what it was, more than anything else, was the pulps: cheap mass market magazines named after the vile paper on which they were printed, published weekly, biweekly, or monthly, sold for five or ten cents a copy, and snapped up eagerly by audiences eager for colorful short stories. Pulp magazines weren't new in the 1920s, but the conjunction of cheap magazine production and the effective mass marketing of short stories through corner newsstands hit critical mass in that decade and benefited science fiction and fantasy tremendously.

Mind you, these two genres made up only one corner of the pulp market. There were Western pulps, romance pulps, Western romance pulps, mystery pulps, adventure pulps, "spicy " pulps (which danced as close to the edge of erotica as you could go in those more prudish times without violating the postal regulations), and so on through a dizzying array of genres and sub-sub-sub-genres—but science fiction and fantasy had their own lively corner in the newsstands where pulps were sold. The sheer volume of stories demanded by the pulp industry meant that quite a bit of garbage and even more mediocrity saw print, but it also made room for a remarkable burst of creative innovation. Though of course there were important earlier works in both genres, most of what we now think of as science fiction and fantasy can trace its roots straight back to the pulp era.

After the budding and blossoming of the golden age, in turn, both genres went to seed. Paper rationing during the Second World War didn't help, but a lot of the trouble was simply that science fiction and fantasy had run themselves into a pair of well-worn ruts. Both by and large turned inward, creating fan subcultures that circulated stories via not-for-profit fanzines and devoted their time to savage quarrels about issues that didn't matter one iota to anyone outside the airtight circles of the cognoscenti. To be sure, some pulp magazines stayed in print, some books saw print in both genres, and some very good stories and novels were written, but a great deal of science fiction and fantasy in those years stuck to lines sketched out in the pulp era, catered to a narrow circle of aficionados, and raised barricades against the world outside.

Then came the paperback revolution of the 1960s. Paperback books weren't new in the 1960s, either, but the conjunction of inexpensive paperback binding and mass marketing hit critical mass in that decade, and science fiction and fantasy both benefited at least as much as they had from the pulps. Publishing houses used to turning out expensive hardback editions discovered that they could boost sales by orders of magnitude with cheap paperbound editions. The stunning financial success of the US paperback edition of J.R.R. Tolkien's *The Lord of the Rings*, which had racked up only modest sales in hardback, and a flurry of lesser but still lucrative bestsellers, opened the eyes of publishers to the huge market for cheap imaginative fiction, and the boom was on.

I was born in 1962 and started reading science fiction around 1969, so the paperback revolution framed my discovery of the genre and nearly all my early explorations in it. Not just bookstores but grocery stores, drugstores, and department stores all carried science fiction and fantasy paperbacks—I bought my first copy of Roger Zelazny's Hugo Award-winning *Lord of Light*, for example, in the paperback section on the top floor of Seattle's Bon Marché department store, and my first collection of Robert E. Howard stories, *Sowers of the Thunder*, in a Rexall drugstore a dozen blocks from home. The sheer volume of imaginative fiction churned out by paperback presses in those years guaranteed that much of it was garbage and even more was mediocre, but it also guaranteed that astonishingly innovative visions could find a home in print.

Then, like the pulp boom, the paperback boom peaked and began to ebb. The paperback industry remained as vital as ever—visit your local supermarket and you can count on finding a rack of paperbacks as gaudy as anything that ever graced a 1970s grocery store—but once again, both genres had run themselves into ruts. Science fiction fixated on a narrow range of potential futures, fantasy on an even more narrow range of imaginary worlds; book sales, and the number of new books published in each genre, declined accordingly; and both genres once again turned inward, creating fan cultures that circulated stories on not-for-profit websites and devoted their time to savage quarrels about issues that didn't matter one iota to anyone outside the airtight circles of the cognoscenti. To be sure, some paperback SF publishers stayed in print, some books saw print in both genres, and some very good stories and novels were written, but a great deal of science fiction and fantasy in those years stuck to lines sketched out in the paperback era, catered to a narrow circle of aficionados, and raised barricades against the world outside.

Then came—but before we talk about that, it's probably worth taking a moment to talk about the ruts.

Where science fiction is concerned, the deepest of those ruts is the interstellar future—the notion that the rest of humanity's history will be defined by expansion into interstellar space. It so happens that there are solid reasons to think that nothing of the sort will happen, but let's set that aside for now. The point that I'd like to make is that as a theme for science fiction, it's been overdone to the point of dreariness.

Was the interstellar future worth exploring? Sure, back in the day when it was still new and interesting, but that was a long time ago. At this point it's hard to think of a more shopworn cliché in the genre—for heaven's sake, it was already old hat in science fiction novels and short stories when the original *Star Trek* TV series premiered in 1966, and that was, ahem, fifty years ago. Yet year after year, novel after novel and short story after short story regurgitate yet another round of rehashes of the interstellar future, as though it's the only game in town.

And it's not the only game in town, not by a long shot. Futures of interstellar expansion are only one small subset of the range of possible human futures. There are countless vivid, imaginative, interesting futures out there that don't happen to be cluttered up by starships, and such futures used to be all over science fiction. They'll be all over science fiction again, and so will many other novel and interesting things, once the genre levers itself up out of its rut, and starts exploring futures that are genuinely *different*.

Another rut worth mentioning is the way that the great majority of science fiction these days assumes that our kind of industrial society, complete with all its most parochial features, is the template on which every future human civilization is going to be built, no matter how far in the future you care to look. You saw that really rather odd assumption in older science fiction—Isaac Asimov's *Foundation Trilogy* has a really bad case of it, set in a galactic civilization so far in the future that the inhabitants thereof have forgotten that humanity originated on Earth, but who still talk and behave exactly like Americans from the 1950s—but you also saw futures that differed as dramatically from our present as our present differs from the ancient past.

Cordwainer Smith's stories of the Instrumentality of Mankind are a classic case in point. Meeya Meefla in the era of the Rediscovery of Man may share a location and a time-rounded name with the present-day city of Miami, Florida, but a brief stroll along Alpha Ralpha Boulevard in the former city will cure you of any tendency to confuse the two. In Smith's vision, the future really is a foreign country; they do things differently there, and it's a safe bet that the habits, customs, beliefs, and worldviews any human society five thousand years from now will differ from those of present-day industrial society at least as much as these differ from those of ancient Egypt or Sumeria five thousand years in the past. Too often nowadays, that gets missed, and science fiction is the poorer for it.

The deepest of the ruts that afflicts fantasy these days, on the other hand, isn't defined by a theme. It's defined mostly by the creations of a single author. Yes, that would be J.R.R. Tolkien, whose novels loom over most subsequent fantasy fiction like the Lonely Mountain over the Desolation of Smaug. Before Tolkien's great trilogy hit the big time in the 1960s, fantasy fiction ranged over an extraordinarily wide range of tones, themes and imagery—compare

Robert E. Howard's "The Queen of the Black Coast" with George MacDonald's "Lilith," or H.P. Lovecraft's *The Dream-Quest of Unknown Kadath* with William Morris' *The Well at the World's End*, and you've got some sense of the dizzying reach of fantasy back in the day.

Once B.T. (Before Tolkien) gave way to A.H. (*Anno Hobbiti*), on the other hand, though there have always been authors who tried more or less successfully to do other things, Tolkien's themes and certain derivative spinoffs thereof (cough, cough, *Dungeons and Dragons*™, cough, cough) became the endlessly rehashed clichés of an entire industry of derivative fantasy. I'd encourage readers who doubt this to ask themselves this: how many fantasy novels have you read set in worlds where the characters wear cloaks, are governed by feudal monarchies, wield straight crosshilted swords, shoot with longbows, and can be neatly divided up into *Dungeons and Dragons*™ character classes, even when they don't happen to fraternize with elves, dwarves, and dragons? How many white-bearded wizards with long robes, pointy hats, and magical staffs does it take to change a stereotype? And of course there's the ultimate rehash of rehashes, the most enduring and least interesting thing Tolkien contributed to the genre, the generic Dark Lord.

To be fair to Tolkien, his Dark Lord wasn't generic. When Sauron first appeared on the horizon of fantasy with the 1949 publication of *The Fellowship of the Ring*, the concept of an antagonist reduced to pure negation, a monstrous shadow projected against the skies of Middle-earth, was extraordinarily novel. The difficulty was that it didn't stay that way. Go through any collection of paperback fantasy these days and you'll find Dark Lords under every enchanted rock, all of them fitted out with the usual gear: here's the sinister fortress, there are the spooky messenger-huntsmen, there are the legions of doom, and somewhere else is the magic Macguffin that the protagonists have to find or wield or steal or lose or destroy or otherwise manipulate in order to save Lower Upper Outer Southeast Central Earth from the evil plots of the local Dark Lord. You can practically check the contents off on the packing slip.

Oh, and does the Dark Lord have any actual motive for those evil plots? Of course not. He's doing it all because he's evilly evil for the sake of pure evil evilness, with a gallon or so of evil sauce poured on top. At most, he's got a backstory that's supposed to explain how he managed to rise to his current condition of evilly evil evilhood. Tolkien, again, was doing something specific and interesting with his Dark Lord; he reduced the antagonist of his story to an incomprehensible darkness so that, against that stark background, he could explore the complex moral and personal choices by which all his characters, the heroic, the humble, the tragic, and the villainous, defied the Shadow or crumpled before it.

Recycle that through an endless sequence of derivative fantasy stories, and what you get is much more predictable and, frankly, much duller. The Dark Lord pops up, cackling on cue, to frighten the bejesus out of everybody; the protagonists line up meekly to join the Fellowship of the Macguffin, and set out on the inevitable quest to find or wield or steal or lose or destroy or otherwise manipulate the magic Macguffin in order to thwart the Dark Lord and keep everything exactly the way it was at the beginning of the story. If you're really on top of your clichés, of course, the main protagonist is a hopelessly misunderstood adolescent who happens to be the only special snowflake in Lower Upper Outer Southeast Central Earth who can do whatever it is with the magic Macguffin, but that's an assignment for extra credit. A long string of overfamiliar incidents duly happen, the protagonists win, and the story grinds to its inevitable halt, if you've gotten that far before dozing off.

Fantasy used to be more interesting than that. Some of it, fortunately, still is. Meanwhile, the poor elves, dwarves, dragons, pointy-hatted wizards, heirs of ancient kingdoms lost or simply misplaced, Dark Lords, and the rest of the generic-fantasy crew have been working forty-hour weeks plus overtime for many long years now, and I'd like to suggest that it's time to throw a big retirement party, hand out the gold watches, and pension them off. Now's an especially good time to do that, because the next publishing revolution is already under way.

Print-on-demand (POD) publishing isn't new, of course, but the conjunction of cheap POD printing and effective internet marketing seems to be approaching critical mass as I write these words. Ten years ago, certainly, I couldn't have counted on finding a small press like Founders House, the publisher of this magazine among many other things, to release an anthology of science fiction stories set in futures where industrial civilization has peaked and declined like the civilizations of the past—much less four such anthologies so far.* The

* These are *After Oil: SF Visions of the Post-Petroleum World* (Founders House, 2012); *After Oil 2: The Years of Crisis* (Founders House, 2015); *After Oil 3: The Years of*

enthusiastic reception given to those anthologies and my novel *Star's Reach*—another work of deindustrial SF, in which industrial civilization has proven to be a temporary dead end, interstellar travel turns out to be impossible, and radio communication with other worlds is the only form of alien contact the future will ever hold—leads me to think that the POD revolution, like the paperback revolution and the pulp revolution before it, is having a familiar effect on science fiction, breaking down the ruts and widening the range of imaginable tomorrows by many orders of magnitude. Publications elsewhere, most of them also from POD presses, give me a great deal of hope that the same process of expansion has begun to reshape the landscape of fantasy fiction as well.

If that admittedly speculative prediction is correct, readers of science fiction and fantasy stand at the brink of a new era of wonders, equivalent to the golden age of the pulps in the 1920s and 1930s or the great fantasy and science fiction boom of the 1960s, 1970s, and early 1980s. An torrent of new fiction, given free rein by way of POD technology, will once again find a much larger audience and take both genres in directions we haven't yet dreamed of.

Renewal (Founders House, 2015); and *After Oil 4: The Future's Distant Shores* (Founders House, 2016).

The masterpieces of that era haven't been written yet, and the themes that will give them their power may still be hanging out in whatever green room of the collective imagination shelters such things before their hour on stage. There will inevitably be plenty of trash, and even more mediocrity, but if I'm right, we can also expect great works of science fiction and fantasy that will forever reshape their genre and be read for decades or centuries to come.

That won't last forever, of course; in twenty or thirty years, perhaps, systole will once again give way to diastole, science fiction and fantasy will settle down into whatever the next set of ruts happen to be, the barricades will go up once more, and fans will again busy themselves with savage quarrels about issues that won't matter one iota to anyone outside the airtight circles of the cognoscenti. In the meantime, though, we may just have a golden age to get through.

CLOSE CONTACT

BY D. A. D'AMICO

"**W**e have a hugger!" The cop flipped a clear Lucite shield over his respirator, checking his cuff guards where they joined thick rubber gloves.

Airi Komatsu cupped the filter tight over her mouth, her eyes scanning the courtyard. People scattered. Bright rubber hazmat suits squelched as terrified shoppers waddled quickly into puffer locks along the promenade, leaving Airi alone with the policeman.

"I hate this part." Her husband had asked her to find another line of work, but they needed the money. Little Aiko wasn't even two months old, and there were so many expenses with a new baby.

She felt naked. The paper suit rustled as she tugged it snug against the rubber sheath underneath. She struggled to control her breathing, her heart fluttering, the antiseptic tinge of mint flavored filters burning her throat.

"There he is! Be careful."

It happened fast. He came out of nowhere, undressed except for street clothes, his wide face unshaven and unmasked. He stumbled, falling against the polished flooring, his bare hands striking the patterned tile in greasy slaps.

"Please, let me hold you..."

"Ryo?" Airi gasped, backing away from her brother, unable to believe her eyes. "What are you doing here? I haven't seen you in months. What's happened to you? "

He looked terrible. Small cuts covered his hands and arms, smears of blood still clinging to uncovered skin. His face appeared blotchy, eyes sunken, skin sallow and dragging over high cheekbones. He trembled as if cold, but the summer sun hung high above lush treetops.

"Sister." He bowed, strangely formal.

"You know this guy?" The cop readied his pacifier rod, putting himself firmly behind the big gripper arms.

Airi nodded, still too stunned to react. She'd never expected to see her older brother here, not like this, not so vulnerable and afraid. Ryo had always been the rock, the keeper of tradition. He'd run the family after their parents had died. He'd sent her to school, got her settled in her first job, kept her safe until she was able to make it on her own.

"Why?" Airi steadied her face mask, one hand held out as if warding off evil. "What makes you want to kill yourself? "

"I'm so alone..." He stood, arms outstretched. His gaze darted from Airi to the policeman.

He took a step closer. The cop jerked the pacifier at him, and he pulled back.

"Relax, you're not alone anymore." Airi's soothing tone sounded choppy, words broken by the hiss of her respirator. "I'm here for you. I've always been here for you. "

He held out his naked hand. "I need to *feel* the warmth of another living being. Touch me."

"That's not going to happen." The cop circled, looking for an opening.

Airi gave the officer a dirty look. "Don't worry about the policeman. Talk to me, Ryo. Why didn't you come to me? I could've helped. I could have done something."

"Like what, hide behind your respirator and hope you didn't catch anything? "

"It's not like that."

Ryo was Airi's third hugger in as many months, and he wouldn't be the last. Incidents were on the rise. Institutions were filling up. The media blamed modern medicine for creating ever more resistant strains of bacteria, but scientists were still baffled. Airi only knew it meant more heart breaking confrontations like this one.

The human microbiome, the unique and invisible cloud of bacteria surrounding each and every person, had become toxic. The host remained immune. People were not in danger from themselves, but the simple act of close contact had become deadly.

"We're going to get you some help, Ryo." She tried to hold his attention as she moved away from the officer. "I work with really great people, and we'll do whatever we can to find a cure for this."

"I'm not sick, and I don't need doctors." He moved closer. She let him, hoping the policeman had circled far enough around.

"You can't think this is normal, can you?"

"It's the way nature intended, no rubber, no plastic, just people. " He reached out, dirty fingers nearly touching the fringe of her oversuit. She had a sudden flash, an image of his microbiome as a layer of steam hissing towards her.

She cringed, but tried not to run away.

"We're not animals, Ryo." Nature could never have intended the human body's bacteria to suddenly prove hostile, but it'd been a part of life for nearly three generations. Society had adapted, but some people could not.

"No, but we're not really human anymore, are we?" He lunged forward.

Airi scurried back, but her brother was faster. He grabbed her. She screamed. Rough fingers shredded her paper oversuit, caressing the thin plastic beneath as his arms wrapped around her. His cheek brushed her face mask, raspy, scraping the clear plastic like a wire brush. He pressed against her ear. She held her breath.

She struggled, her gloved hands slapping at his body, the heat of contact making her sick. He squeezed. She vomited, the stench and moisture clinging to her respirator.

"Get off her!" The cop snapped the pacifier, jerking Ryo back as the device spun a cocoon.

Airi fell to her knees, gagging. "Don't hurt him. He's ill, not evil."

"Yea, right."

"That's perverse…." Jimmy Yamashita glared at the screen from behind a clear triangular mask. Ancient video played, a woman and a little boy walking down a path lined with blossoming cherry trees, no hazmat precautions, no gloves, holding hands. They stopped in front of a school. The woman knelt, and the boy hugged her. Airi glanced away.

"It's work related. I'm researching causality, trying to get a handle on these huggers." Airi lied. She didn't know what had drawn her to that file.

She was still shaken from her encounter. Finding her brother like that had left her off balance, almost dizzy. The police had scoured the scene. Paramedics had cleaned up her torn outfit and ruined breather mask, but there was no way she could wipe the images from her mind.

She tapped her desk and the video vanished.

"Is he in holding?"

"They brought him in after they hosed him down." Jimmy tugged at his finger cots, absentmindedly snapping the rolled edges where bone-white rubber gloves met black latex.

"Good." Airi adjusted the airflow on her backup hood, the reek of vomit haunting her like a bad memory. "I'll check in before I go home."

She stood, but Jimmy blocked her path. "Remember, you're a social worker, not a psychologist. You can't fix him."

"There's two to a room!" Airi marched into the holding area, her face flush, the soles of her rubber slippers screeching with every step. "There's hardly any screening. They can practically touch each other."

"Take it easy." Noriko Sakai moved like a mermaid, soft flowing steps drawing her across the polished tile floor. She wore a thick rubber oversuit with a clear cylindrical helmet. Her long black hair hung in Medusa braids, framing her round face in snake-like coils that trembled with the flow of air through her respirator.

"They're not animals, you know."

"No, they're not." Noriko lifted a clipboard. Rubber pages flopped like dead fish as she turned away. "But we've had too many cases lately, and we don't have room for everybody."

Airi stared through the large window. Ryo sat on the edge of a thin bed, his hands tied to a restraining bar, his temporary plastic suit like wrinkled skin. He didn't appear as dangerous as he had on the promenade. They'd scrubbed him, shaving his head and dousing him with a pink-tinged antibacterial. Now, he only looked pathetic.

"I'd like to speak with him."

"Be my guest." Noriko nodded at the airlock.

Airi stepped in, tugging her long pink gloves up to her elbows and closing her eyes as a brief pulse of ultraviolet filled the screened enclosure, followed by a mist of antibacterial and antimicrobial resin.

"How are you feeling, Ryo?"

He looked up, eyes bloodshot behind the flexible plastic hood as he started to cry. "I want to die."

"No, you don't. You're just confused."

"*I'm confused?*" He tried to stand, but fell back. "What's the point of all this? What are we living for, if not to be close to each other?"

He yanked the restraints, twisting the plastic sleeves until they bunched up around his pale grey gloves. When he couldn't move anymore he started moaning, almost growling, as he jerked against the bed frame.

"Trouble?" An orderly pushed through the airlock, a slimmer version of the policeman's pacifier in his thick gloves.

Airi waved him away, turning back to Ryo.

"You said you needed somebody to touch. Why?"

"Are you a monster? " He stopped struggling. His eyes were wide, panicked, and he gasped as he spoke as if the words were suffocating him. "Can't you feel it, like magnetism? It's instinct, it's *biology*. We were born tactile, but it's been hidden away like it's something filthy."

Airi rolled a small stool close to the bed. She trembled, suddenly cold. Ryo looked so much like the man she'd grown up with, but something had changed in his face and eyes. He'd become someone else.

"We're conditioned from birth to take the danger of contact seriously. Not just you and me, but *everyone.* You know how wrong it is, but you don't seem to care. Why? What's changed?"

They'd grown up together. Airi remembered a dashing young man full of hope and eager for the future. He'd been so full of life. Where had that man gone?

He sighed, lowering his face until his plastic mask touched his chest. He looked forlorn, his expression so saturated in despair she wanted to cry.

"How can any of us really be alive if we're sealed off from the world?"

They hadn't spoken much since the news of her pregnancy and the birth of Aiko. Ryo had no one else in his life. There was nothing to ground him, nobody to keep him from feeling alone. He was adrift in a world where each man *was* an island, and Airi felt it was somehow her fault.

She reached for his hand, but pulled away, horrified. She'd almost touched him.

"I have to go." Her heart pounded, her face hot with shame. She jumped from the stool so quickly she slid against the second bed. An elderly man glanced up, his expression the mirror of Ryo's dejected features.

She wandered the streets, confused. So much had occurred in the last few hours, so many questions racing through her mind. She felt scared. Loneliness pressed in on her, but she knew it would be impossible to talk about this to anyone. Physical contact was taboo. People wanted to pretend it never happened, and it was worse because it had happened to her own brother. She'd be suspect by association.

Traffic was light, no autos and few pedestrians. Couples strode the immaculate porcelain streets, keeping a respectful meter apart, rubber oversuits squelching as they lumbered in the late afternoon sun. Airi passed children in their bulbous clear hoods, faceplates obscured by mist because they hadn't yet learned how to breathe properly. Would they ever live in a world where they could feel the breeze on their faces, unafraid and free of filtration and thick germ barriers? Would she?

She thought of Ryo and her own upbringing. Had there been something missing, some flaw making him susceptible to erratic and dangerous behavior? It'd been nearly a decade since the fire that'd taken their parents. In all that time she'd never seen the signs, never suspected anything wrong.

Seeing Ryo in that hospital room had made her second guess her whole life.

"You should've called me." Hiro stood at the door screen, arms crossed over his light evening oversuit, a thin cloth mask covering his pinched features. He wasn't happy.

Airi knelt beside the crib, watching little Aiko's hands stretch the thin plastic membrane, eager to escape. She'd had a hole in her heart since Aiko was born. It ached, the feeling something was missing inside her. Now, with Ryo's breakdown, she worried she might know what that might be.

"It was my *brother*. You can't know what it's like seeing him like that." She'd come straight to the nursery when she'd reached home, hoping to avoid the inevitable confrontation, the accusations. Hiro had never liked her job, and he'd never cared for her brother. Now he had an excuse to hate both.

"You have to change careers."

"Do I? Why?" She turned. He stared at her, his expression withdrawn. He felt so distant, as if there were more than just a few layers of plastic between them. "I can help him, Hiro."

"Have you helped any of the others? Has anyone?"

"What am I supposed to do?"

He stared at her, his eyes shifting back and forth as if he could penetrate her mind with his gaze. "I don't know, but I think you should stay away from him. In case..."

"In case what?" She stared back, trying to mimic his heated gaze. "You think I might be like him, don't you? You think I could *become* that one day."

She'd started to wonder the same thing herself, but seeing it in her husband's eyes made it real.

Hiro glanced at the baby.

"No, no..." Airi moved to block the crib, her heart racing. "How could you even think like that?"

Hiro pushed off from the wall, letting his arms drop. "Ryo's just looking for attention, and you fell for it. You care too much."

"Who else is going to care!" She shouted it.

The baby started crying, and she turned to sooth the little girl. When she turned back, Hiro was gone. She could hear him in the bedroom. The hissing rustle as he inflated the outflow canopy meant he'd be going to sleep without waiting for her, angry again.

He'd become colder since the baby was born, as if he'd thrown up an extra layer of insulation between them. She had hoped it would pass. She'd hoped he'd adapt and learn to open himself up, but he'd just become more detached.

The baby fussed, and Airi rocked the crib, wondering if the world would still be as cold and sterile when her daughter grew up.

"Hush, my sweet." She slipped her hands through the openings in the crib's glove box. "*You* love mommy, don't you?"

Could Hiro be right? Was she at risk, and would this somehow affect their daughter?

Airi waited until the sounds from the bedroom stopped, and then slowly lifted the holding frame from the crib's corners. Aiko poked at the membrane, her tiny face radiant, her eyes wide and attentive as Airi pulled the plastic sheeting back and removed her gloves.

"I wish things were different..."

She held her naked hand above the crib, palm down. The baby's tiny arms flailed, clutching at air, struggling for contact.

"I wish I could hold you and let you know how much I love you..."

She could feel the unshielded warmth from the little girl's body, but couldn't bring herself to touch her own daughter.

She cried silently beside Hiro most of the night, sick at the loss of something she couldn't understand. It felt like an ache deep in her stomach, an itch she couldn't reach. The world seemed suddenly empty.

It got even worse as she scurried through the pedestrian tunnels on her way to work. Individuals lumbered by in thick hoods, their faces hidden, their bodies shapeless lumps. Very few people spoke. Rubber shoes squeaked, plastic suits crunched and crackled, respirators wheezed, but there was no laughter, no interaction. Everything seemed flat, as if her life had been squeezed between the plates of a microscope.

"Why so glum?" Noriko slid across the floor, her thick oversuit and tall hood identical to the day before. Her Medusa braids waved as she nodded in the direction of Ryo's room. "He's awake. Go ahead."

Airi tried to control her breathing. She needed to know what was happening to her. She needed answers only her brother could supply.

"Thanks. I won't be long."

Noriko stepped in front of her. "Doctor Watanabe evaluated your brother this morning. He's troubled, but not dangerous to himself or others. It's a mild case, and he stands a very good chance at recovery."

Airi nodded, quietly entering the room.

The bed opposite Ryo's was empty. She didn't know if it had anything to do with her complaints, but it gave her an opportunity to speak in private.

"I thought you'd come." Ryo sat awkwardly on the floor beside the bed, his oversuit resting like a tent on his body. They'd taken the restraints off. His arms were free, and it made Airi a little nervous.

"You did?"

"I could see it in your eyes." He stood slowly, backing up to the bed. "You feel it too."

"Feel what?"

"Let's not play, Airi. We're alike. I know when you're unhappy, and I know you won't let something go once it gets in your head. You're wondering if this could happen to you, admit it."

"I'm not sure." The air inside Airi's hood felt uncomfortably hot. She loosened the drawstring at her throat. "Maybe."

He laughed, the sound robotic as it hissed through his hood's respirator. "Give me a hug."

"No!" She tensed, but he made no move.

"Then there's nothing wrong with you. You're perfectly *normal.* Go, live your sterile life in peace."

She panted. She saw spots before her eyes, and it felt as if the air had stopped circulating through her helmet. The tension sat like a rock on her chest. "I have a daughter, Ryo. I need to be sure, for her sake."

Her left glove had an ornamental quick release tab. She pulled it, wiggling her fingers free. It felt surreal to hold her naked hand in public, and she trembled as she waited for Ryo to touch her.

"This isn't you, little sister." He didn't move, but his smiled sagged. "You aren't a monster. Your daughter *will* grow up healthy and normal, so stop testing yourself."

"Please..."

He hesitated, staring into her eyes. Then he shrugged and removed his gloves, rubbing his hands together. They made a shuffling sound, like the pages of a book. Airi held her breath. Her hand shook, but she didn't pull away as he slowly reached for her.

"I can't!"

She screamed. She jerked back, falling over, scrambling away. Her vision wavered as if she'd been submerged deep underwater, and she felt sick. What was she doing? Hiro had been right. She'd gotten too close, let empathy affect her judgment. She cried, slumped there on the ground like a rag doll, arms in her lap, her head down so she didn't see when Noriko and the tall orderly rushed into the room.

"Ryo..."

Airi glanced up. Her brother crouched against the wall, his hood hanging loosely from the collar of his oversuit like a second head, his arms flailing. The orderly dodged, ducking under Ryo's swing with a practiced grace, and he plunged the pacifier tongs against Roy's torso. The device spun, wrapping a cocoon of sterile silk around her brother.

Noriko knelt, her face against the shield of her helmet, a wisp of fog where her lips kissed the plastic. "Are you okay? He got your glove, but did he hurt you? "

"He didn't..."

"Good." Noriko backed away. Airi had been about to say she'd taken her own glove off, but the woman hadn't given her a chance.

"Do you need help? I can get a lifter."

Airi shook her head and struggled to her feet. "I'll be okay. I'm just stunned."

Ryo whimpered. He'd been sedated. They'd wrapped him tight, leaving only his head exposed before maneuvering him onto the bed. He looked pathetic, stiff and unnatural, like a mannequin in a sack.

"I'll get someone in to re-mask him." Noriko whispered to the orderly, and the man stepped through the airlock.

"May I stay for a few minutes?" Airi hugged herself, her uncovered hand hidden beneath the folds of her oversuit. "

"Sure." Noriko shifted her gaze from Airi to Ryo. "He won't bother you again. I'm really sorry about that. We were told..."

"Don't worry. I understand."

Noriko nodded, and followed the orderly out.

Airi stepped close to the bed. Ryo lay completely still, more than just asleep. He looked almost peaceful, and she wondered if he would ever fit back into society, ever be able to enjoy a sunny day without wanting to tear his suit off.

He had a niece he'd never met. Maybe with more love in his life he might not feel as desperate and alone. Maybe they both wouldn't. His recovery would be a long road, but Airi'd be there to help.

"Get well, brother." She ran her naked hand quickly across his cheek before stepping out of the room.

QUARANTINE

BY D.B. KEELE

They had been toiling their way up the mountain for three days when they found it. And not a moment too soon, for the crew was growing weary of slaving away with no indication that they were any closer to progress than when they disembarked onto the beach and watched their vessel retreat into the sunset.

That first night they set up a make-shift camp far enough inland to avoid the tide, and spent the night inside small tents, eating only dried fruit and jerky. It was not worth risking a fire yet, as they had no idea if the island was still inhabited, and if so, by whom... or what. Nathan had lain awake into the night, mind racing. It had been five years since the last crew had been dropped off, and that was the last anyone had seen of them. Before that, another crew had disappeared into the jungle, but of that group, one man had remained when the time came for their extraction crew to pick them up.

Miller had always been slightly unhinged, with his theories of ancient civilizations, lost tribes, supernatural beasties, hidden treasure, and all the other trappings of the slightly paranoid, book-smart but jungle-stupid archaeologist that he was. But by God he had been a brilliant man. He had isolated this small island from a handful of legends, scattered about in journals, manuscripts, scrolls, and scraps of maps that basically amounted to "go not here, monsters there be..."

Few would listen to him expound upon his whacky theories, but those that did, usually late into the night and a few sheets to the wind, would find themselves slowly reassessing their entire world-view. Slowly beginning to consider... what if, just what if this madman is right about everything? Most would then chuckle, take another swallow of the brown stuff, and walk away shaking their heads. But then there was the one man that Miller won over. And really, in the end, the only man that counted. He was Ezra Smythe, of the Smythe Trading Company. And Ezra Smythe was filthy stinking rich, and not afraid to put up a little capital for a crazy theory, if the potential payoff made it a worthwhile risk.

So on that night ten years ago, when Miller met Smythe at the Bloody Monk Inn and Tavern, it was surely fate, God's will, or the Devil's sense of humor, take it as you will. In any case, the dreamer and the schemer came together over mugs of ale, and history was set in motion. Miller had been holding forth with a small group of colleagues from the university, when Smythe sat near their table to be close to the warm fire crackling away in the hearth.

"By God, I tell you, it exists. It exists as sure as this oaken table upon which we rest our mugs, gentlemen. And I know where it is. All I need is a proper backing, a writ of mission from the church, or a wealthy financier with deep pockets. And of course, a crew brave enough to join me. We will find it, map it, document it, and within bounds of propriety, loot it. Aye, it would be a shame to leave such treasures festering in some tropical jungle, surrounded by naught but savages and beasts."

"Miller, yer' a loon. T'ain't nothing out there where ye keep pointin' yer bony knob of a finger on the map. I've been at sea. I've been long at sea, and ain't nothin' there, 'cept a pack o' lies the boys tell back home to get the ladies breakin' out in goosebumps, and needin' a bit o' comfort."

"Damn it, Jenkins, you're not listening to me. It's there. You don't know squat, save what the king wanted you to know back in your navy days. I've done the research, I've compiled the tales. White gold, jewels, the treasures of a lost civilization, abandoned during a great plague. The natives on surrounding islands still tell the tales of those that came before. The Marked Ones, roughly translated. They were a different race, a larger, paler race, that came upon the sea. They settled the island and dominated it, enslaving or driving out the natives. But then, as legend tells it, they angered the gods.

They unleashed a curse, some kind of plague, and it began decimating their kind, and even the beasts of the jungle began to suffer. A few made it onto escape vessels, but those were never heard from again. The natives on surrounding islands speak of the treasures left behind, vast treasures, vast stores of knowledge of an era gone-by. Thousands of years, laying in wait, for someone with the knowledge, the bravery, and the skill, to plunge into that dark island and make off with it. I am that man, Jenkins. And you can go straight to hell if you think I'm going to give up on this."

"Ah, bugger off, Miller... let's git boys, there are less crazed tables we can visit, with livelier conversation, and maybe a lady or two..." With that, Jenkins and his motley crew scooted back their chairs on the rough-hewn wood floor, chugged the dregs of their drinks, and departed in search of more desirable company.

Smythe had been listening to all of this, of course, and once the doubting Thomas and his friends had wandered off, he gave Miller a moment to feel the depths of his abandonment before making his approach. He sat thoughtfully by the fire, stroking his great mustache, smirking as he considered the absurdity of what he was considering. Coughing, he stood up, shook out the chill still in his bones, and approached Miller, who sat dejectedly staring into his empty mug.

"Mr. Miller, I take it? May I buy you another ale? I'd like to hear more about this island of yours..."

And they were off to the races.

Of course, Nathan had learned of all of this in his debriefing before launching as captain of the current team. Smythe was more determined than ever to successfully explore the island, and recoup the costs of the previous two missions, as well as that currently being incurred for Nathan's expedition. It would seem a fool's errand at this point, save for Miller having survived the first one. When the extraction ship had arrived, they had come upon the beachhead at night, and cast the anchor down, while spying the rocky shore with a spyglass. There seemed to be something strange there on the rocks, but it was too hard to make out. A two-man dinghy was sent to row to shore, with lanterns and torches. What they found has itself become the subject of legend.

There on the beach was arrayed a sight straight out of a nightmare or perhaps a scene from hell. There was some sort of tableau arranged there in plain view on the dark rocks, consisting of human bones. The remains of four, maybe five men were there, constructing some Byzantine design that to this day no one is sure what was intended. The men lifted their torches and looked out into the dark jungle, looking for some further sign. Seeing none, they approached the bones, and as they walked closer saw a glint of something shining there amidst the macabre scene.

Young Jones bent down, and upon closer inspection, found that it was a single bottle, stoppered with a cork, containing a rolled parchment. Removing the parchment, he read the message by the glowing lantern they had placed on the rocky shore. "Come not into the jungle at night. Stay onboard, I will make myself known by the light of day. All our safety depends on this. MILLER."

Jones and Bay stuffed the parchment back into the bottle, climbed back into the dinghy, and as they proceeded to push off and row back toward the mother ship, as they tell it, they heard an inhuman, feral moan that caused the hairs on their neck and arms to stand straight up, and a shiver to travel down their spines. They've tried to describe it, mimic it, point to known creatures as examples of what they heard, but to no avail. They merely say a mournful, menacing moan that was followed by more of the same. Even as they describe it to this day, they shiver.

Come morning, the boat was sent ashore once again, this time manned by two other men who were not terrified by the moans heard the night before. By the harsh sunlight, the remains on the beach seemed less menacing, but no less horrific for what they seemed to indicate. Only Miller remained from the previous crew, and perhaps only long enough to compose that parchment, then wander off into the jungle to die himself. As the men stood contemplating this, a crashing sound emanated from the jungle. As they prepared to pull their pistols from their waistbands, they looked up and saw a Wildman burst forth from the greenery, long hair and beard flowing, wearing nothing else save the shaggy hair, and some kind of amulet.

"Run! Run, you fools, to the boat! I am Miller! Wait for me before shoving off!"

His shocking and sudden appearance coupled with the events of the night before, compelled the men to take him seriously, and so they ran and jumped into the small boat. Soon Miller, the naked bearded Wildman, came tumbling into the boat as well, foaming at the mouth and screaming at them to "Cast off, you bloody idiots, or it will surely have us all!!!"

And cast off they did.

Once back at the main vessel, it was soon ascertained that Miller was mad as a hatter, and potentially bearing some plague, running a high fever, and refusing food and water. His emaciated form was quite different than the shape he'd taken when dropped off the previous year. His eyes were the eyes of a terrified beast, awaiting the hammer and blade at a slaughterhouse. His skin was burning to the touch, and covered in bruises. And yet, there was the amulet. The amulet was like none the crew had ever seen. It was clearly some form of pure white gold, comprising a chain, and a large pendant of the same, with a massive ruby enshrined in the midst. Miller refused to remove the thing, and spit and clawed at any who tried to remove it from him. Thinking he was potentially contagious, and yet worth something to their employer as a source of information, the crew dared not harm him in any effort to remove the thing.

Their only mission had been to extract the original team, lead by Miller. These men were neither trained for, nor capable of an advanced exploration of the island, and besides, Miller had been, and remained, the only reliable source of information about what treasures the island may contain, and where they may be located. And being as he was now in their care bearing the proof of treasure around his neck, it was decided that the best course of action was to quarantine Miller and the two men he'd been in contact with below decks and get them back home as soon as possible for Smythe to do with as he pleased. As for the rest of the original crew, they had to be presumed dead and decaying there on the beach. And so, they departed, watching the mysterious island disappear into the mists.

Miller was dead before nightfall. This further convinced the crew that he was bearing some plague. There was some talk of removing the amulet and throwing him overboard, but no one wanted to go into the room where he'd been locked and touch the corpse. So it was sealed up and left untouched until they arrived at home port. Smythe was notified, the remains, and amulet, were recovered by his representatives. The two men that had borne Miller to shore in the dinghy never fell ill, were remanded to their own custody, and paid a bit of extra hazard pay for their trouble.

Of the second crew, there is not much to tell. They were given some top-secret information by Smythe, presumably derived from knowledge he had gained from the mysterious amulet, left on the shore five years after Miller and five years before Nathan, and never seen again. The rescue ship arrived by daylight, scouted the shore, found no sign or trace of the crew. They remained anchored offshore for five days, in case the crew had been detained in reaching the pickup point, but no one ever appeared. There were reports of mournful moaning, inhuman howling, and spectral glows at night, but no signs of any survivors. After the fifth day, the captain had no choice but to depart without them.

Smythe had approached Nathan after one of Nathan's lectures at the University. He had heard rumors about Miller, of course, but since everyone had always assumed he was basically a paranoid lunatic, not much was thought of his death while out chasing down legends. Smythe asked Nathan to his estate for dinner, and after dinner laid out the details of Miller's expedition, the one that followed, and Smythe's intention to back yet another expedition to the island. He wished for Nathan to lead that expedition.

Nathan was amused at first, but then as the conversation continued, he became intrigued. He felt an odd sense of urgency developing to take Smyth seriously. Smythe excused himself from the drawing room as Nathan enjoyed the warm brandy he had been offered. He gazed into the flames of the fire and considered what a strange world this was, and how anything is possible... is it not?

"Here, sir, is the artifact. Only I and my counsel in this matter have seen it. I keep it locked in a safe location here, which none save I know, so don't get any ideas about coming back for it after hours. Haha..."

Smythe was bearing a plush magenta pillow, carrying it with great delicacy, and approaching Nathan from across the room. Even from a distance, Nathan found himself entranced by the wonder of such an object. The white gold glistened like pure snow under the fire light; the ruby was the deepest red, a gulf of blood to lose your sense of time gazing into. Smythe placed the pillow on the table near the fire with care, and drew back to gaze down at it.

"This, sir, is the only thing that proves that Miller was not just a crazed maniac who devoured his crew and ran through the jungle buck naked for a year with no good cause. Miller was right. There is something on that island. Something important. My counsel has assured me that this amulet is quite ancient. It bears little resemblance to anything he has ever seen. It is the purest gold and largest ruby he has ever assessed. And the writing on the back...oh, yes...the engraving..."

Smythe carefully turned the amulet over, revealing the large expanse of gold that encased the ruby from behind. Upon the gold was an etching...some kind of script. Beautiful, elegant...and utterly alien to Nathan.

"Anyway, he assures me that this is a language, though no language that he has ever encountered. It bears no resemblance to any current language, though he thinks it may share some relationship with some of the Scandinavian dialects, to his closest estimation. At any case, this makes what is already an invaluable piece of jewelry and history, completely unique and utterly priceless. And for all we know, it is the first of thousands of its kind. All we need is to find where on that island Miller located it. And that, sir, is where you come in."

Nathan was confounded. He had come here this evening expecting a nice meal, some great liquor, and a tall tale to laugh about as he lay down to sleep. But here he was, heart racing, considering taking up this Smythe on his offer. And not for any love of riches, but my God, an undiscovered civilization? An unknown tongue? This was the stuff that did not happen anymore. And it was his to learn, his to explore, his to write about.

"Mr. Smythe, you have my attention..."

And then after a whirlwind of preparations and the long journey at sea, Nathan had found himself laying in the tent on the beach that night, lost in thought and unable to sleep with anticipation of the day ahead. Unfortunately, any thought that Smythe had some arcane knowledge to guide them with derived from the amulet, was of course mistaken. He'd send the second crew based only on where Miller had departed the jungle foliage, the sheer existence of the amulet, and the promise that it held. Miller's corpse, or what was left of it when the ship arrived at port, had been cremated immediately. No one else ever fell ill, and that was considered the end of any potential plague. The second crew had vanished into thin air. And yet, Smythe had spent years stewing on the matter, and keeping his eye out for someone with the talent and knowledge to perhaps complete the mission that Miller had begun.

Smythe had pegged Nathan as that man, and Nathan had been willing to chance it, based only on the amulet and the tale surrounding it. He had of course tracked down some of the men on the first extraction ship, to corroborate what Smythe had told him, and ease his mind that the amulet was not some expensive fake created at the whim of Smythe to lure him into the mission. The story he heard was the same over and over again. The men's shivers when recounting the moaning and howling heard from the shore seemed genuine enough. And so he chose to believe, chose to risk, and signed on for the mission.

He lay awake that first night, and listened for disturbing noises, and found that he was almost disappointed when they heard none. Human nature is a fascinating thing.

The first day, the crew packed up as dawn was breaking, and began their attempt to penetrate the jungle to discover her mysteries. He and Smythe had decided on a small crew of five, just as the first crew lead by Miller had been. As badly as things had ended, it had still resulted in one man surviving for a year, and the only evidence of any success making it back to port. So five men it was. Nathan had hired his army buddy Jacob, and between the two of them they had compiled the best team they could, considering the risks involved. They were lucky to have anything other than convicts willing to go.

They spent twelve hours hacking their way through dense foliage, assaulted by an ungodly heat, humidity you could soak dishes in, and every insect you could imagine, and a few you can't, attempting to feast on their life's blood. It was hellacious work, and it seemed with the incline they were working their way up and those obstacles, they had their work cut out for them. That evening a great rain descended from the distant mountains, and they all huddled under the trees and their tents, attempting to stay dry, teeth chattering. How is it that a boiling furnace by day can become miserably cold by night? At least the rain kept the insects at bay that night. The jungle was eerily quiet, the peace broken only by rainfall and the occasional rolling of thunder.

The second day was more of the same, with the added discomfiture of sore muscles, sun burn, and swelling insect bites incurred the day before. The crew worked in silence, grim, but determined. At some point, the terrain began to thin out into smaller shrubbery and tall grass, having reached some kind of plateau on their way up what was proving to be the base of a great mountain. The men took comfort in the easier pace they were able to keep in this setting, though the occasional sighting of a quickly slithering serpent kept them on their toes. The spiders that scrambled out of their way were the size of small cats, and probably ate the same fare.

They stopped at the base of a new incline near dusk, and set up camp. That night was dry, and the air was somewhat lighter since they had reached a higher altitude. The night air was full of loud fluttering and high-pitched shrieks, as massive bats swooped overhead. Nathan reassured the men that they were after insects, not their blood, and as such were their friend on this journey. This was only slightly reassuring, since the creatures were large enough to carry off a small child. How many insects could satiate such a beast? The men snuggled into their tents for the night, ready to dissolve into unconsciousness.

Their slumber did not last long, for once the moon was high, the sounds began. Nathan was first aroused by a low guttural moan in the distance that made his skin crawl. It was surely just some jungle cat, or possibly an unknown primate, but by God if it didn't sound like the wailing of the damned in hell. He poked his head from the tent and found the others doing the same. Jacob looked at him and sucked in his breath, as if to indicate, "Well, boss, here we go…"

"Pay it no mind, men. I'm sure it's nothing. Let us get whatever sleep we are able, and by first light of day, we continue our climb."

Little sleep was had by any that night. The moaning continued occasionally, and it was joined by twittering, cackling, and what sounded like footsteps in the brush around the camp. Once again, Nathan told himself it was probably just some unknown primate, probably a type of spider monkey, and the moaning was the jungle cats that hunt the poor creature. At any rate, by the time they all emerged from their tents the next morning, yawning and rubbing their bloodshot eyes, it was clear that day three was going to be their greatest challenge yet.

And the morning was a miserable one too. The men were grumbling, nipping at each other over nothing. No one was much motivated to do much but put one foot in front of the other, occasionally hacking down some plant that was in his way. They stopped for lunch when the sun seemed to be overhead, seeking some shade amidst a grove of small trees. As Nathan sat consuming his meager rations, most of the men did the same in a small circle. There was no small talk, only ragged breathing, chewing sounds, and the occasional cough. Jacob was restless though, and began walking around, poking his machete through the weeds. And then he yelled out…

"Boss! You'd best get over here. I think I found some sort of cave entrance…"

The hole in the ground was about half the size of a man. Nathan had to crouch down to gaze into it. There was a slight draft coming from the opening, he could feel it tickle his beard. He called for a torch to be lit and brought to him. Once arrived, he held it out into the opening and sure enough, the flame flickered from the slight breeze. He could see nothing but darkness as the opening descended into a greater recess of some kind. There was a slight odor on the breeze coming out of the cave entrance. It was stale, and yet… fetid.

Nathan turned to the men, and in hushed tones said, "Well, men, this may be it. We may have found something here."

Jacob led the first team down, taking two of the others with him. They tied off a great coil of rope, looping around each man's waist, and tethered outside the cave to a great boulder. Nathan and the remaining crew member, Embry, took watch outside the cave entrance. The men descended into the opening with lanterns, slowly making their way down the tunnel as it gave way to pitch black. For a while, Jacob was able to yell back to Nathan with what they discovered, nothing much remarkable, a wet hole in the rock, with the occasional pale newt scurrying out of their paths.

Nathan yelled down into the chasm, "I can barely hear you now, Jacob... we will keep watch outside and give you two hours time to make your way as far as possible and back, to report on what you find!"

Nathan and Embry lingered around the cave entrance, making small talk and sweating under the already blazing morning sun. Nathan updated his captain's journal, as it were, with the discovery of the cave and the initial exploration attempt. Embry dozed a bit leaning against a large boulder, and Nathan decided not to chastise him. It had been a long, sleepless night and when the others got back it may well fall to he and Embry to descend next.

After the two hours had elapsed, Nathan began to grow concerned. He leaned forward into the cave entrance, holding out his torch. Nothing but that stale breeze. He yelled down, "Jacob, what goes on? Can you hear me?" No response.

"Embry, I cannot stand it any longer. Help me hoist this rope and try to gain their attention."

The two men grasped the thick rope and began to tug it upward, expecting resistance. They found none, the rope quickly coiling up at their feet as they worked. Nathan tried to hide his anxiety as they worked. After some time, the frayed, snapped end of the rope came to rest at the cave entrance. Embry turned to Nathan, lips pursed, eyebrows raised, and exhaled slowly.

"Well, Embry. This is troubling. Let us prepare to descend and search for our crew."

The two men were silent as they made their way down the shaft, grunting occasionally as they squeezed through the tight spaces. Nathan's skin crawled and he let out a yelp once when a massive translucent spider scampered across the back of his hand. He was not a big fan of confined spaces, nor arachnids, so suppressing the girlish scream he felt inclined to release required great strength of will. Embry took no notice of the event, and they continued their descent.

After what seemed like hours, the shaft began to open up into a greater chamber. Nathan rested against the wall and lifted his lantern high. It pierced the darkness in a small semicircle around the two men, and Nathan risked shouting, "Jacob! Williams! Howard! Can anyone hear me? Embry and I have made our way into the first chamber. We need to return to the surface before nightfall and our lanterns run out of fuel!" His words echoed back to him, with no response.

Embry began to make his way past Nathan, holding his own lantern aloft. He worked his way along the chamber wall, cautiously, breathing heavily. "Boss, the air down here is rank. We can't stay too long. Our lanterns are burning lower due to lack of oxygen. Perhaps the others fell upon some grave misfortune, and we are next?"

Nathan closed his eyes and leaned back against the cool rock. Exhaling slowly through his nostrils, he began to feel a panic rising up in his chest. Has he led these men to their doom? Will another extraction team arrive to find nothing but the blank silence of an empty beach?

"Boss! I've found another chamber..." Nathan opened his eyes and saw the faint form of Embry as he began to walk into the black hole in the wall. And then he was gone.

"Embry? Embry? Damn it, man!"

Nathan scrambled over to the hole in the rock through which Embry had disappeared. There was an odor wafting out of the opening, the stench of rotting carrion mouldering in a wet dark place... Nathan felt goose bumps consume his body as he raised his lantern into the blackness ahead. He stepped through the opening.

***I** am that which waits. At last one has come into my domain that is found worthy. And now I wait again. Eons spent in the lightless hollow tomb in which the others encased me, though not before I contaminated their bloodline and assured their extinction. The other was more fortunate and discovered the talisman preventing my embrace. I hungered. I consumed. And now this one came, after I had strengthened myself on the flesh of his fellow men.*

And I wait again. This form is weak, and lacks the satisfaction of my natural state. I miss the malleability of my true self. The oneness with my surroundings. Tentacles exploring, expanding, contracting, consuming. But there is a price to be paid. Assuming this form allows that which I crave most. Escape. This rock amidst the sea has encircled me for far too long. It is time that I roam the earth once more. The spells cast by the ancient ones held me here in my true form, but this thing, this man, allows me to pass through the barrier.

I wait. This shell will be sufficient. When the vessel comes, I will be here. I will be here. And they shall suffer my wrath.

HUMANITY

BY JOANNA MICHAL HOYT

The old man sat bolt upright, biting his lips and waiting for his trial to begin. He had always hated speaking publicly as a civilian; he didn't know what to do with his eyes and hands; and now the stakes were terribly high.

He didn't expect to save his own life. He had fought with the resistance at the end, had held his own for a long time against greater numbers and better weapons, and he'd pay for that. But if he could command any respect or sympathy, if he could intercede for his friend and co-defendant, the doctor, who had never fought...

Above the bench where his judges would sit were carved the words posted in every public building in every world of the diaspora, the final words of the Great Pledge they all repeated daily: "TO PRESERVE AGAINST ALL MENACE FROM WITHOUT, ALL DISSENSION FROM WITHIN, OUR COMMON AND PRECIOUS HUMANITY." That was what he and the doctor and all the Pure had been trying to do.

His advocate, a harsh young man appointed by the court, had dismissed this argument. "Stop posturing. Let them see that you're old, frightened, *human*. For humanity's sake don't quote your omnipestilent Commander." The old man hoped his judges would prove more understanding.

The judges filed in. Thick-skinned, small-eyed, squat men and women shaped by generations of Ipiu's harsh atmosphere and fierce insects. None of them were beautiful like his people, shaped by Arraj's kinder climate before the earthquakes and eruptions forced them to take refuge on Ipiu two generations back.

He joined in the reciting of the Pledge. Like his judges he spoke in the clipped Unic of the Interworld Consortium. He might have solaced himself with the rolling cadences of Arraji, but he needed to remind his judges that they were all humans united against the common enemy.

An evidentiary declaimed the list of accusations.

Breach of the Code of Humanity—well, the Code was always interpreted by the party in power.

Land seizure—how could they claim that? The Ipiu had acceded to the Arraji's request for a new homeland as the earthquakes devastated Arraj, and the Arraji had never tried to take anything beyond Andek, the barren and *esur*-infested continent allotted to them.

"Murder; gross inhumanity; cruelty to noncombatants, to children..."

The old man rose. He knew, now, what to do with eyes and hands and voice.

"You must not slander us so! My people have never killed or mistreated children or other noncombatants. Only your soldiers—and a few medics, I suppose—invaded our adopted homeland. None of your children came there. If they had come we would not have harmed them. We never attacked your medics...some may have been accidental casualties of our self-defense..."

Judges, advocates, evidentiaries, reporters, stared at him in apparent bewilderment. Perhaps they were mistaken, not lying. What had they heard?

"We have never neglected our duty toward children and unfortunates. I chaired the Arraji Children's Aid Board before you destroyed their headquarters and confiscated their funds. I contributed more than my share to the Interworld Relief collections; you have paralyzed or destroyed our databanks, but if the lines of communication ever open again to the Interworld Consortium their records will bear me out." He took a deep breath, remembered his priorities. "But I am only an ordinary man, doing as all the Pure did. As, no doubt, Your Honors do. My co-defendant is a more striking case. He has devoted himself to medical research for the good of humanity. He has always been a noncombatant. He has a wife and a small son who are now deprived of his assistance, presence and comfort. Is this not cruelty to children?"

"Are you mad?" the old man's advocate hissed.

"No. Are they?"

An evidentiary rose to speak.

"With the Court's permission, we will begin by itemizing the evidence against the defendant who has just interrupted the Court's proceedings."

"Objection," the advocate said.

"No objection," the old man said.

The evidentiary held up a small black-bound book.

"Do you recognize this?"

"Yes."

"What is it?"

"My personal duty log from my time as a sanitary coordinator."

"You entered this information yourself? You can vouch for its correctness?"

"Yes."

"I will now show the Court an entry from this book. You may inform us if it has been changed in any way."

The old man nodded. The blank wall at the end of the court lit up, showed an enlarged image of a notebook page covered with his cramped Arraji next to a typed Unic translation. "Ejeget, 6/17. Standard sanitary operation. Pestilentiaries thermoconverted: 137 mature male, 245 mature female, 44 juvenile male, 56 juvenile female. Energy profit: 46 amplissae."

"Is this entry correct?"

"It is." So many days, so many sites, how could he remember? But it was plausible, and there was nothing there that could be used against him.

"You still deny killing children?"

"Of course I do!"

"Would you tell the Court what you did in the process of this 'sanitary operation'?"

"My unit and I were sent to Ejeget by my superiors. Upon arrival we found the *esurin* verified and isolated in a warehouse at the edge of the town. They were too close to human habitations for thermoconversion—exudates might have compromised air quality. My men removed them to a quarry which was abandoned, stripped of useful material, and well downwind from the town."

"Go on."

"The *esurin* were marched into the quarry. One rank of my sanitaries stood at the lip of the quarry, prepared to shoot any who offered interference. The rest set up the thermoconversion booth, moved the *esurin* through in groups of ten and interred solid byproducts. Then the booth and battery were removed and we set out for the next town on our list. We encountered no children."

He stopped, thinking.

"No, I had forgotten. There was a young girl, the daughter of a woman who after the daughter's birth had been seduced by an *esur* in our collection group. That girl ran after us, shouting. Two of my sanitaries returned her to her mother. She struggled violently, so her wrists may have been bruised, but there was no cruelty."

"No cruelty, either, to the children who died in your thermoconversion unit?"

"I tell you, there were no children! To thermoconvert humans would be a clear violation of the Code of Humanity. We would never—I would never—have condoned such a thing."

"Then how would you describe the—juveniles—you killed?"

"They were not children! Not humans! All of them were *esurin*. This was manifestly obvious in most cases. A few were more... well-disguised... those who had interbred with humans, to our shame and to the danger of humanity—but the selection specialists were highly trained and conscientious. All those collected for disposal were *esurin*."

"You have used the Arraji word *esurin* several times. Can you not find an appropriate word in Unic?"

The old man frowned. Linguistics had never been his strong point.

"*Esurin* is one of the true names of the Destroyers, the Children of the Lie. They are not human, though they may appear so to the uninformed. There is no exact translation in your language. Your translators have rendered it as 'pestilentiary", which is close, but..." He turned toward the doctor, who was better at such things.

The doctor caught his glance, rose, and explained.

"'Pestilentiary' is often employed as a figurative term of abuse. Even in the literal sense your pestilentiary is a victim of circumstances, someone who is infected through no fault of his own and who infects others unwillingly. '*Esur*' is always used literally. An *esur* is by nature diseased, and he deliberately spreads disease to humans. His goal is the destruction of humanity."

"This is how you define all non-Arraji?"

The old man shook his head. "No! You Ipi are humans like us."

"And on what grounds do you claim that this is not true of the Verekei?" The evidentiary gave the *esurin* their false-name.

The answer was too obvious to speak. The old man felt his knees buckle.

"Adjournment requested. My client is unfit." His advocate's voice was flat.

"Adjournment granted."

In the hallway the doctor came up beside the old man and looked at him with concern before his guards hurried him away. The concern, the old man knew, was not about their impending sentence or the success of the Lie but about his unsteady gait and ragged breathing.

Finally alone, the old man tried to pull his thoughts together. How could he make them see? He could remember pieces of the speeches of the Commander of the Pure, but he could not recall the words, the tones, that had woven the pieces together into a clear and damning whole.

There was history. The *esurin*, who were resettled on Andek along with the Arraji, claimed asylum on the grounds that their population on Verek was being decimated by a fatal and highly infectious respiratory disease caused by an organism native to the planet. They complied with quarantine procedures before entering Andek. But they had lived four generations on Verek before the disease was identified. If it had been genuine and planet-specific, it should have struck the first settlers. At first some of the Arraji had suspected the disease was a fabrication, a way of claiming sympathy from Interworld Relief and acquiring land on a planet more centrally located than Verek. (Some of the *esurin* had the gall to draw parallels with the exodus of the Arraji, but that was a different matter; the earthquakes and eruptions that rendered Arraj uninhabitable were verifiable; those who said they resulted from

Arraji fuel-extraction operations were politically motivated liars...) When the first generation of refugee *esurin* lived and died in apparent good health on Andek these suspicions seemed to be confirmed.

Afterward, when the gut-wasting sickness struck the Arraji and some of the *esurin* also pretended to be stricken, the Commander recognized the truth of the situation. The *esurin* were creators of diseases, which gave them excuses to move into closer proximity to humankind and weapons with which to destroy them.

There was anatomy. The *esurin* might claim that their large eyes with bloated pupils and shrunken whites, their translucent skin under which the veins showed blue, resulted from living underground to avoid the sickness on Verek's surface, but after the Commander's artists' work was publicized who could fail to see that these were clear marks of the alien nature of the *esurin*?

There were the loathsome crimes of the *esurin* that the Commander's investigative units had uncovered. Not content to wait for their sickness to destroy true humanity on Andek, the *esurin* had stolen human children and killed them. The *esurin* had denied the crimes and alleged a lack of evidence, but the investigators were Arraji of clean descent and good reputations who would not have lied.

The old man repeated the arguments until they were fixed in his mind. He would explain in the morning...

In his dream he was out of prison at last. He walked in sunlight on a high ridge, looking down onto a forest. The breeze sent shivers of silver and shadow through the leaves. Why had he never stopped to see how beautiful the world was?

He couldn't stop. The men with the guns hurried him along, hurried the others along in the line behind him. He went down into the shade of the trees, to the edge of the old quarry. Something down there was throbbing loudly. He didn't want to know what it was.

A harsh voice told him to keep going down. The stairs were steep, he wasn't sure of his balance, but he had to go down or they'd shoot him, he'd fall into the people below him, they'd fall. He went down. Saw the thermoconverter. Kept going. What else could he do?

The thermoconverter's door opened. The charging chamber was empty. He was in front. If he didn't walk in they would drag him as if he was an animal or a *thing*, not a human. He went in, set his back to the wall, turned to see who was with him. Just before the terrible light and the pain began he recognized the doctor.

He woke, sweating and shaking, dressed with unsteady hands, returned to the courtroom. Entry after entry was read out of his book. The evidentiaries refused to call the *esurin* by their proper name or to admit their inhumanity. When he tried to explain they interrupted him. His advocate did not intervene. At the lunch recess the old man called his advocate for a conference.

The advocate stared at him, looking belligerent even for an Ipi. The old man stared back.

"Why do you not object when the evidentiaries refuse to allow me to explain the basic premise of..."

"You have already done yourself enough harm. Your so-called explanations would make things worse if that were still possible. Your chances..."

"I understand that I will almost certainly be executed. I am merely attempting to clear my people and my cause of the slanders which have been advanced against us. And also, if it is possible, to save the life of my co-defendant—an obvious noncombatant—my friend—the doctor." He did not say 'Who is young enough to be my grandson, dear enough to me to be the son I never had.'

"I am not here to salvage your delusions. I'm charged with saving your life if that is possible. You haven't made that any easier." The advocate half-smiled. "Or maybe you have. Let me change your plea. Let me argue that you're mentally unfit. It may even be true."

"No! I do not want to live because of a lie. For myself I want justice or nothing. For the doctor..."

"Justice!" The advocate rose as he spoke. The old man half expected a blow. His guards had hit him before. He didn't cringe.

The advocate dropped back into his seat. "Don't ask for what you deserve."

"May I ask for a chance to speak?"

"Not at the evidentiary stage. They've almost finished questioning you anyhow. They'll be starting on your—*friend*—this afternoon. But defendants may make a final statement before sentencing. If you want the slightest chance of living you'll let me make it for you."

"No."

They watched one another in silence until a guard came to take them back to the courtroom.

When his turn came the doctor explained that he had researched possible cures for the gutwasting plague, which had spread among the Arraji to such an extent that the eradication of the *esurin* alone did not guarantee control. To that end he had requisitioned juvenile *esurin* for experimentation, since the worst devastation of the plague had occurred among Arraji children. The doctor's account was carefully brought down to a level which his hearers could understand. His advocate interrupted his explanation of the similarities and differences between *esurin* and humans to remind the court that the children (as the advocate called them) whom he requisitioned would surely otherwise have been thermoconverted.

"That may be," the evidentiary said. "As some of his victims did not die, we have summoned one of them to appear in court during tomorrow's session." The advocate's hands clenched. The court adjourned.

The old man looked for the doctor as he was led away, but the guards kept them separate. He walked grimly upright to his cell. He slept and he dreamed:

He was in the field headquarters of the Southeastern Sanitary Campaign along with the doctor. This was at the beginning of the end; there were rumors of an Ipi invasion along the northeastern seacoast, but these had not been confirmed, and the old man had not yet begun training his sanitaries as soldiers. The coordinators discussed the rumors, still only half afraid. The old man, listening, envied them, pitied them, and then forgot them. There, across the room, looking out the window, was the doctor. He didn't know that he was marked for death. The old man didn't plan to tell him. He only wanted to sit beside his friend once more, to talk about music, mountains, mathematics, all the lovely things that endured. He started across the room.

One of his colleagues asked where he was going. He turned to answer, but the words froze on his lips. Her voice was his colleague's voice, her uniform and her hair were right, but her veins showed blue under her skin, her eyes bulged obscenely—*esur!*

He recoiled, trying to see who else had seen, who might help him. All through the room eyes turned toward him, horrible distorted eyes. She had infected them all with something far worse than the gutwaste. She had turned them into *esurin*. He had to warn the doctor, to get him away before he also was destroyed.

If he took another step he would be able to see himself reflected in the window. If he spoke the doctor would turn toward him. He didn't want to see the doctor's face, nor his own.

He woke up cold and rigid. He sat up on his cot and tried unsuccessfully to put together some words in the doctor's defense.

He dragged himself into court for the testimony of the juvenile *esur*. The ushers treated the juvenile with the gentleness due to a human child, stood close enough to it to be contaminated. It took its place between the old man and the judges, facing the judges. It looked, from behind, very human, very young. The old man swallowed hard and silently recited the Revelation of the Commander of the Pure which he and his sanitaries had repeated daily along with the Great Pledge:

The esurin *are Children of the Lie. They practice to deceive. Their aim is the destruction of all human life. The torch that was kindled on the Mother-Earth, the spark that gave light to the worlds, they would extinguish. We must not fear them. We must not believe them. We must not pity them. When they are destroyed the wasting diseases will leave us. Fear, cruelty and shame will leave us. We shall be fully human again. We shall have peace. But until we are free of them there will be no peace. Therefore let us devote our time, our resources, our courage and our strength to the work of Purification. Let us never falter in our resolve to preserve against this worst of menaces our common and precious humanity.*

The old man remembered the first time he had heard those words, listening to the transmitter beside his brother, who had turned gray-haired and silent after his child died of the gutwaste, and his cousin, who had been gray-faced and voluble since the *esurin*'s excessive-resource-consumption complaints to the Interworld Consortium closed the mine where he worked. He remembered the hope in those words. His cousin nodding. His brother's head lifting.

The young *esur* spoke in halting Unic.

"I saw that doctor when I was in the...the bad place. They had away taken my mother and my father. I was alone with strangers except my cousin. I asked where were my parents and they didn't answer." He stopped, his lips quivering. "My...my aunt says they're dead. A bad way dead." He gulped and resumed in a higher voice.

"They took us to a hospital, but before I had only to go to hospitals when I was sick, and I wasn't then sick, only scared. They made us line up. My cousin went into the room front of me. I heard him yell. Then they took me in. That doctor was there, in a suit that covered him all over. He weighed me and measured and asked my age, and then gave me a shot. It hurt much, but I did not yell. Then they sent me into a room with beds and no windows. My cousin was there and I sat with him and I told him shots were not to be afraid for and he told me my favorite story about the astronauts. We went to sleep."

He paused, looked down, continued,

"I woke up because my cousin was screaming. When I touched him he was too hot. There were other ones screaming too, or crying, and one shaking so all her bed rattled. So I knew they were sick. My mother said always to watch for sickness and tell her and she'd call a doctor. I couldn't tell her, but I'd seen the doctor. So I banged on the door and I yelled and I said now there are sick people here and you need to help and he didn't come, and so I thought maybe it was night and he was gone home, but I looked and found a camera in the ceiling and I stood right under it and said the same thing and then I thought he would come and I went back to my cousin and I said someone would help, and he said no, and I thought he was crazy from the fever, so I told him about the astronauts while I waited for the doctor to come, but he did not come."

The old man sat with his head in his hands, remembering his nephew tossing in the fever, screaming, then growing silent. Remembering his brother, smiling at the boy, telling him he would feel better soon; weeping, singing a lullaby; stone-faced, staring at the boy's body.

The young *esur*'s story went on. The housekeepers shoving trays of food in, slamming the door, not listening to the boy's—the *esur*'s—pleas. The orderlies coming in their protective suits, taking temperatures, drawing blood, giving nothing. Telling the boy, when he kept asking why, that they were the control group. The fevers, the screaming, the vomiting, the stench. Many deaths, including the cousin's. Then, finally, the three children who had not sickened and died being taken away for more tests under the doctor's supervision. Kept in another room for a week, monitored daily, having blood drawn, screaming at night from dreams not sickness...

"Are you all right? Can you hear me?" the advocate asked quietly. The old man realized that his head was down between his knees. He couldn't straighten up. He couldn't answer.

"You're ill. I'll call the guard to take you back to your cell."

The old man rose, lurched, grasped at the guard's arm. The guard recoiled. The old man fell. Someone lifted him, bundled him into a wheelchair, rolled him away. He kept his eyes down, not wanting to see the disgust on the guard's face again, not wanting to look at the doctor and feel a similar spasm of disgust crossing his own face.

That night he dreamed. He ordered a file of *esurin* into the thermoconversion chamber; one looked back at him with his brother's haunted face. He ordered that an example be made of an *esur* who had attempted to interfere with a collection, and found himself staring at the doctor's mangled body. He didn't notice at first when his victims stopped changing, remained clearly marked as Verekei. When he did notice his sick horror did not abate.

He called his advocate in.

"Have you decided to let me make your final statement for you?'

'No...that doesn't matter. I needed to tell you..." The old man groped for adequate words.

"You've already told me that your *friend* deserves to live. I'm not defending him. His advocate is doing what little can be done."

"No...not that. I had to tell you...I know now...I did not know before, but I know now, that the...Verekei...were human." He had said it. He had broken the First Law of the Pure. The voices in his memory screamed at him: *Traitor! Corrupter! Hater of true humankind!* Newer voices, too sure for screaming, called him worse and truer names.

"So you've decided it's safer to admit that after all? And you think this...revelation...will impress the judges? It's too late."

"No! It isn't calculation, I...I did not know and now I do. Too late to save them..."

"You never knew?"

"No! We were told...we were all told..." So they had been. Even before the Commander's rise to power. He remembered the taunts when he failed a test, the scoldings when he was cross with his younger brother. *Don't be such a verek!*

"What do you want now?"

"To confess. To apologize."

"This is not your time to speak in court."

"Must I go back and listen while I cannot speak?"

"No. Your part of the evidence is concluded. Let me know if you change your mind about your statement."

The old man nodded. The advocate left.

The next day was bad. The old man swung between cold horror at what he had done and furtive self-pity for his ignorance. First his statement sounded groveling, then cold, then merely stupid. The night was worse.

Back in court the next day, he listened while the doctor's advocate spoke unhopefully of the duty of victorious nations to be merciful. He stood when his time came to speak.

"I can say nothing in my own defense. My actions were indefensible. I have told this court what I believed, that the... Verekei were not human, that our campaign against them was waged on behalf of humanity. I know now that I was horribly wrong. I did not know then, but that does not excuse what I did to my... fellow humans. Nothing can do that. I am guilty of murder, indeed, and of defamation as well. I apologize to those Verekei who survived." He swallowed. "I submit myself to judgment. Whatever sentence I receive, it can be no worse than my actions have deserved. But I ask you to have mercy on my co-defendant, who shared my ignorance, and whose actions, however misguided, sprang from his love for humanity."

He looked at the judges, who stared coldly at him. He looked at the doctor, who did not seem to see his friend at all.

The sentence was death by thermoconversion. Publicly broadcast. In three days.

His advocate walked into his cell unannounced.

"It's over, then. Unless you wish to make an appeal."

"I do not. You are not sorry."

"Should I be?"

"Not for me."

"For humanity?"

"You loathe me. Why did you agree to defend me?"

"You never saw, did you? You stood there explaining the self-evident inhumanity of the Verekei, and you never saw what I was."

"You?"

"My paternal grandfather was Verek. He came to Iberra for a scientific conference and met my Ipi grandmother, stayed there to raise his children, left his son there to marry another Ipi, went back to Andek himself as an old man. I have my mother's features. I was in law school on Iberra when we got word that my grandfather was dead. Accused by your Commander of atrocities he never committed and sentenced to death in a sham trial, with no advocate. Then you were taken. No one wanted to defend you. I couldn't bear to have it said that you were killed unjustly like my grandfather."

The advocate left abruptly. The old man looked after him, shook his head, activated the viewscreen in his cell; anything to take his mind from memory and regret...

His own image was all over the newsfeeds, together with images of the doctor and the Verek child. Some of the images were photos. Some were 'artistic renderings' which caricatured the slenderness of the Arraji, made him and the doctor look more like insects than men, and gave them expressions that were anything but human.

Ipi commentators and decision-makers, speaking in solemn and elevated tones, discussed the ramifications of the case:

The trial had set a clear precedent for sentencing others complicit in Purification. Mass executions would be more energy-efficient, since so much power was required to activate the thermoconversion unit.

The serum which the doctor had developed showed some promise against the gutwaste. It would be given to the surviving Verekei and, preventively, to the Ipiu presently on Andek, and to other Ipi if they chose to settle there to relieve the overcrowding which had begun to trouble Iberra. It would not be given to the Arraji. Why should they be allowed to profit from torturing children?

The ideology of Purification had spread throughout Arraji society, tainting even those who had not taken an active part in the sanitary campaign. Clearly that ideology posed a fundamental threat to humanity. In view of that threat, might it not be necessary for humanity's sake to eliminate the threat prophylactically?

The old man deactivated the viewscreen and stared into the dark. When he could find words he sent a message to his lawyer: *Have your people decided that we all are* esurin? *Have you been infected by the madness that possessed us? Where will it end? Can none of us help ourselves?* The lawyer did not answer.

He tried to write to the doctor, could not; he didn't know whether he was writing to his friend or to a true *esur*.

A fragment of memory came back to him. The doctor, very early in the sanitary campaign, midway through his struggle against the gutwaste, sitting exhausted at the old man's kitchen table, talking, not meeting his friend's eyes. "Humanity. Did you know that in the source-language, on Old Earth, the word meant two things? They used it for the species, as we do, but it had another definition. It also meant kindness."

"They used the species-name for kindness? On Old Earth, where they killed each other over pigmentation and metaphysics?"

The doctor stared at his friend, stalked out the door. He did not turn when the old man called to him. The next day when they met the doctor apologized, saying he had been distraught after the death of three more patients.

The old man sat up straight on his prison cot, pulled out the tablet they had given him, wrote a halting message to the doctor recalling that night. He gave it to the guard to deliver. It was returned, unopened, by the same guard, who said that after hearing the old man's pre-sentencing statement the doctor had refused to receive messages. Since then he had not spoken.

The last morning came. The old man greeted it with relief. The only thing he had left to hope was that Ipiu would be a dead planet before its links to the Interworld Consortium were restored, before the plague he had spread could reach beyond Ipiu. He walked out quietly between his guards.

The doctor walked ahead of him, half carried and half dragged by guards. They reached a flight of stairs. The doctor's feet dragged, caught. He lurched forward. The guard on his left let go of him. The other guard swung round and took the doctor's weight before his head could hit the stairs.

The old man saw the brief convulsion of pity on the guard's face and the hard look that came down over it. He stared, remembering.

He and the doctor sat in the park on a sunny spring morning two months after his nephew died despite the doctor's efforts to save him, two weeks after the first speech of the Commander of the Pure. They did not discuss death or politics. The doctor talked about a new fugue he had heard, whistled a piece of the theme. The old man nodded, listened, smiled; started when the shouting began.

A Verek man ran past them. A crowd of Arraji pursued him, shouting. Someone threw a stone. Then another. The Verek raised his arms to shield his head, stumbled, fell. The crowd fell on him.

The old man sat staring, cursing himself for a coward and an *esur* because he did not run to the lone man's aid, cursing himself for a traitor for pitying one of the *esurin* who had caused his nephew's agonizing death. The doctor rose abruptly and set off toward a quieter part of the park. The old man went after him, telling himself *It's all right, what could I have done, it didn't matter anyway, he isn't one of us.* He swallowed the Commander's next speech like medicine to cool the fever of self-accusation. In time he taught himself to believe. But he had chosen. He had known.

"Can I speak to my advocate?"

"Too late."

"Not a legal appeal. Just... Can I speak at the end?"

"You'll have a few minutes while the thermoconverter warms up."

They were outside now, in a hard-floored courtyard. One thermoconverter, humming as it began the activation sequence. Two condemned men, four guards, seven judges, one cameraman, and another man. The old man's advocate.

"Your grandfather died alone?"

"Surrounded by men who hated him."

"I am sorry." The old man tried to meet his advocate's eyes, turned away, looked into the camera. "I have something to say. I...In court I said one thing that was true: that the Verekei were human, and that I and mine had murdered them. I said something, also, that was false. That I was deceived. That I had been an innocent pestilentiary. And when I saw that your people were beginning to see mine as *esurin*, to prepare to destroy us before we destroyed humanity, I thought that you were pestilentiaries as well, that you could not help yourselves. But this was false." He swallowed hard.

"I knew the Verekei were human. And then there were the shortages, and the plague, and the communications breakdowns, and I was afraid. My nephew died of plague, and I grieved. I did not know how to save the people I loved, and I was ashamed—I reproached myself with the name I thought was most shameful—I called myself a Verek. Then I heard the Commander blaming all our griefs and shames on the Verekei, and I wanted it to be true. I told myself the Verekei were not human. I did things that made me unworthy to lay claim to humanity. It... It is a word that meant kindness, once." He glanced at the doctor's blank face.

"I chose to kill, to lie. I did not have to. Many of my people did not choose what I chose. It is not a plague, a fault in our race. It is not a plague in yours. It is a choice you make. You must not make it. Please do not do what I have done. Do not make yourselves into what I have become. We are all human, after all...the kindness, the cruelty, the cowardice, the courage...it is for all of us to choose, it is all human...Please choose better..."

The words were still wrong. He looked at his advocate, who appeared almost as blank as the doctor.

"Time's up. Machine's ready." The guard turned him away from the advocate and the camera, pushed him—not too hard—toward the open door of the thermoconversion chamber. The old man turned back toward the doctor hanging limply between his guards.

"Come on, my friend," the old man said. And, to the guards, "Let me take him." He forced himself not to recoil from the doctor as the guard had recoiled from him. He pulled the doctor's arm over his shoulders, leaned into the doctor's weight, moved forward with him. Eight careful steps. One last look back.

Just before the door closed, just before the terrible light and the pain began, the old man saw his advocate's face streaked with tears.

THE NEW WISDOM

BY DAVID SENTI

In the scientific community, skyrocketing suicides were the most dramatic sign accompanying the so-called "Death of Knowledge." It's hard for us to imagine the despair of those days for the men and women in that noble (albeit primitive) profession. For over a century, every new discovery of science was the product of ever-more-complex technological marvels, and the collapse of funding that accompanied society's abandonment of the discipline spelled the end of a long-trod road.

Never mind that long-trod also meant well-worn, such that no great discovery had taken place for fifty years. And that science as an institution had deviated from anything resembling a pursuit of metaphysical truth, despite the best intentions of many of its followers. And never mind that the rash of suicides were all the more tragic for their predictions being so flatly wrong; to the people of the era, human knowledge had reached its uttermost limit. Those who lived for the pursuit of knowledge saw no more point to their lives.

The ancient art of science is now regarded as quaint, even laughable, by our peers, but I don't shower the classical scientist with such scorn. Our New Wisdom is so obvious to us that we see scientists as hare-brained obsessives, poking crudely at the universe with the blunt stick of repeatable experiment. None of us could say that we would not have done the same in the Silicon Age, for they were driven by the same impulse that enlivens us. They searched for Truth—not truths, but Truth. While they didn't find it, their actions found the path. To them we owe a great debt, as the scientist owed the alchemist and astrologer before him.

They dug around the numbers in hopes of figuring out what they were missing, and their men of the method wandered across the beginnings of ours. It was the heretics of their age, however, who'd formed a tangent to the truth with their minds, the Diracs and Eddingtons and Smolins. They spotted a few important numbers where they were supposed to be, like 1/137 and the 120[1] magnitude scale, the mathematically-inclined always annoyed at the lack of integers. The math was beautiful, and the world only almost so. It broke every theory. Eventually their theories incorporated breaking itself as an element of the world, destroying beautiful symmetries to match observation.[2] The rest were caught up in that mad dash that had served them so well for four centuries, a pursuit of unity in the physical, unity in a manner observable by a lens.

Billions upon billions of US dollars[3] were thrown at this aim, while countless geniuses (of an older type) thundered mightily against the limits of thought and observation, all in vain. What was worst of all--what stands out so clearly to our age but was understood by few then--was that they knew it was in vain. They had seen in their numbers and experiments the same things we know today: that the small and the large and the very large follow different laws; that the infinite singularity breaks all laws; that any journey to the extreme of any element of reality ended in madness; that observation itself breaks down at the smallest levels.

Why were they so obsessed with unity? It had served them well in the past, and indeed, the answers we found have a deeper unity to them more beautiful than any they'd known. Yet their methods could not but see the physical and repeatable, such that the disharmony of scale was a madness they could never grant. How does a man accept that the world is nonsense, after all? Nonetheless they lacked the tools to crack it.

Again, the truth was spotted, as if a shadow out of the corner of one's eye, by men of the right temperament and mindfulness. Most were led to abandon that glimmer by their colleagues and observations; not knowing the true Pattern, they would take blind stabs at the proper traits of the universe and invariably come up short. The disappointment must have been palpable. Driven by their scientific method, they had no means by which to pursue that beauty they sought without intellectual dishonesty. And the supposed "Death of Knowledge" in the mid-21st

[1] The Fine Structure Constant and the once-maligned "problem" of the Cosmological Constant.

[2] They actually came to believe (to our bemusement) that reality was the product of nature's *failure* to maintain its harmony. The psychological effects of believing reality itself to merely be the collapse of harmony must have been deleterious indeed.

[3] A pre-modern currency with no fixed value. Don't ask.

century took even that crude tool from their hands.

The later age pinned its hopes on computers to find solutions, but models are only ever as good as their inputs. Computers could approximate based upon human approximations, which is actually not very useful at all for those unafraid of a little work. If anything, it damaged their efforts somewhat by substituting the work of mind and imagination with processing power, which is a poor trade indeed. Processing power does not equal intelligence. Even if that vain hope for "a software of the mind" had been successfully developed, it would've merely shifted the burden of mind and imagination to another, and a mind much less suited[4] to finding the truth of our universe's underlying law.

Van Horowitz was born and educated into this world. We all know the famous story, where he realized that the great numbers could be plotted as a sequence and a line drawn through them to match each to its proper scale. It was, in effect, the last and crowning achievement of the scientific mind, to find its replacement. Observation had shown him that the universe had a pattern of a different sort, at all scales, in all times, and in all things. He had found the Rhythm of Constants. Seeing the pattern overtly for the first time began the sequence that all initiates now undertake, but without any of the guidance that we take for granted. What bravery it took to plunge headlong into mystery[5] without a guide! If any had found it beforehand—and there is much to suggest many had, in the once poorly-understood madness that plagues failed initiations and that they called schizophrenia—none had emerged from the process intact before Horowitz and revealed it to the world. To do so without guidance was reserved to history's greatest mind.

For those not in our field and ignorant to the process, allow me to explain in brief. Looking out into the universe, in any of its elements, we see patterns. Yet these patterns do not obviously tie to one another, and they are never perfect.

Many throughout history noted a parallel between certain patterns,

[4] Any true digital mind would necessarily resemble the recursive network that exists in the human mind, but it would also carry within it all the logical fallacies of man's present understanding, and these hard-wired. Imagine if the intellectual follies of, say, the 10th century had become an inescapable part of our anatomy! How men expected that to actually improve their understanding of the world speaks either of hubris or a lack of introspection.

[5] Though, as those in the Order know, the process is virtually inevitable once the line is crossed, Van Horowitz was not aware of this at the time.

and one in particular was spotted even by the ancients. Called phi or the golden ratio, they had no idea that this ratio was merely a coincidence of their time, where the Fibonacci portion of the Grand Pattern (GP for short) happened to overlap on many scales in our era. Doubtless, had humanity lived a billion years earlier or later (which we know to be impossible, but they didn't), another series of overlaps in the GP would've been just as obvious. The whole of human culture may have varied, with an entirely different standard of beauty, though such thoughts are mere irrational flights of fancy. They saw in this ratio something divine, because it appeared in many places without any seeming explanation. Other such coincidences were discovered with time, but all attempts to connect them failed.

Horowitz saw that there was a sequence of sequences, a numerical (or musical, or visual) Landscape, after discovering that the fine structure constant had definitively shifted over time. By some stroke of genius beyond us, that tiny bit of information sent his brain into a whirlwind of activity, until he generated that first, rough three dimensional map of the GP. As his brain was itself a product of this pattern and comprised of a series of connections governed by it,[6] apprehending the Great Pattern set off a chain of mental events that is inevitable, hard-wired into our minds.

Most notice it first in music, as did he, though some did so in old "random walk" or "complex" patterns like stock data or star maps. Something about it makes sense, but not in a manner that can be articulated. Horowitz then spied it in grass, in people's speech, in cloud patterns, in everything. This inevitably decouples our consciousness from its lifelong reference points while the initiation sequence plays out in the brain. A sort of internal vision[7] takes place that can be extremely dangerous and is not to be pursued outside of our Order; without our guidance, it usually drives men mad. I cannot elaborate much further, but suffice it to say this: the individual sees that the various elements of reality - in time, space, matter, constants, properties, persons, and relationships - is an expression of the GP, cycling at different rates on various scales and dimensions.

[6] This recursiveness, sometimes called "the Pattern-seeing-the-Pattern," is the very mystery of consciousness. As the GP explains the underlying mechanisms behind reality, the most successful mind is the one that can best intuit it. This allows perception of an ever-greater amount of reality internally, until a certain level is reached where the Pattern in the mind is roughly complete. At that point it can "simulate" anything mentally, even the Pattern.

[7] It is more complicated, and there are no actual hallucinations ordinarily, but a vision is the best approximation.

Reality is the sum total of all possible expressions of all possible relationships between all elements of the GP, and we call this the Landscape.[8]

The pre-enlightened thought that computers are particularly well-suited to the task of pattern analysis, once the pattern is known, but it is not so; the human brain, being an exquisite and many-layered expression of the GP, is of itself nearly a microcosm of the Landscape. This expresses itself as consciousness, because it has an innate and emergent ability to refer to itself in a multifaceted manner. Hence any conscious being is, by definition, perfectly suited to apprehend the Landscape once the GP is known. Though it does not render computers obsolete, as they have numerous other uses, their brief stint as supplements to the human mind had passed.

Science, too, had become a relic of a bygone era, as repeatable phenomena were no longer necessary to understand reality, and the GP could be meditated upon directly without reference to the universe's expression of it, save for confirmation. It even explained those places where our physical laws break down, as infinity is the first "set system" of the GP.[9]

As happens at first to all truly great persons, Horowitz was ridiculed as a loon. Scientists didn't much appreciate the notion that their entire way of life had been rendered obsolete, and none believed him at first. Until, that is, he started making predictions that were impossible. He would predict with 100% accuracy the outcome of a dice roll or any other ordinary "chance" event. He predicted market movements just as easily, and the appearance of an unobserved comet.[10] These things may seem like child's play to an initiate in the Order, but to men of ancient science it bordered on prophecy, witchcraft. Flawless predictive power without observation of a chaotic system was impossible to them. Many sat up and took notice, and the laughter stopped cold.

After expressing the danger clearly and forcing the volunteers to sign waivers, Horowitz took twenty men and twenty women to a private location and showed them the GP, an event now called the First Awakening. Incredibly, 38 of the 40[11]

---

[8] The Landscape is larger and more fundamental than the universe, and includes "universes" beyond ours, many of which wouldn't be physical.

[9] All set systems were at infinity at the beginning of the universe; today on other scales, the infinite set system includes the half-life of protons (for a few billion more years), singularities, and the energy potential of empty space.

[10] The long-period comet called Horowitz's Confirmation.

[11] The two women who didn't make it through

successfully navigated the very first initiation with Horowitz as their guide, a success rate that even today is held only by Grandmasters.

Though the human mind (and all minds) is well-suited for contemplating the Landscape, it is nevertheless so complex that it takes a great deal of meditation to uncover new truths. Those first years, though, were a marvel, as all the low-hanging fruit of the Landscape were picked. The most troubling and disruptive, however, was also the most beneficial: the general trajectory of history could finally be seen with some certainty. The field of antehistory was created.

Now, it could not be seen with great accuracy, mind you; this is The Problem of Imprecision, as it's famously known, which is largely unsolvable. The more complex a series of overlaps are in the GP, the more time and effort it takes to discern its precise outcome in the Landscape. Consciousness takes place in a complex system which involves Landscape recursion, and thus is among the most complicated objects to analyze. An individual's behavior can be known with about 90% accuracy with minimal time, but it takes an incredible amount of effort to raise that to 99% or so. Predicting the outcome of collective human action requires that sort of precision, and thus a great deal of effort. It is not impossible to shrink the error bars to a reasonable size, but simply a matter of resources and efficiency.

The results of this analysis—the first collective endeavor undergone by the original Thirty-Nine Members of the Order—shook the world. Decades of political and intellectual leaders had promised a return to the easy energy of the 20th century without delivering. The analysis of antehistory proved once and for all that the age of ease was forever in the past. There was no glorious material future for mankind, no journey to the stars, and no savior waiting in the wings if only he got enough votes.

And the world sighed in relief. Academia was as taken off-guard by this reaction as it was by the discovery of the GP itself (and finally, it must be admitted, learned a bit a humility thereby). They expected riots and chaos. No small few tried to prevent the results from being published. The whole mass of mankind had already known what antehistory declared, of course, and known it for decades. Now all the political lies and exploitation of resource-rich nations could end, as it was all for naught. The final

unscathed are nearly as famous as Horowitz: Erin and Jun, the First Mad Martyrs for the New Wisdom. Erin's mind was lost much like the schizophrenics of old (though her lot was much better than theirs since she had people who could understand her), while Jun's was of the darker sort.

abandonment of the delusion, far from terrifying the world, was incredibly freeing. Only in abandoning the long-dead dream could civilization accept new ones. And with the Landscape and the Order, intellectual progress was no longer cruelly bound to the gods of technological megaworks. All could contribute. Ever-growing material prosperity was seen for the pipe dream that it was, and it was only reflecting afterward that we realized that it was never a particularly good dream to begin with.

Material decline continued, but with the advantage of a degree of foresight. That in itself was remarkable, and revealed the power of doubt in delusion. The world's "deepest thinkers"—that is, those who possessed common sense and could manage 8th grade math—had long foretold decline of this sort, for all the obvious reasons. Men had lived through it for decades by Von Horowitz's day. Others are tempted to grant us the benefit of hindsight, but let's be frank: failing to see where civilization was heading was inexcusable, the product of willful ignorance. No Grand Pattern was necessary to reveal that infinite economic growth was impossible. What it did provide, however, was the death of excuses.

The scientists who had killed themselves at the "Death of Knowledge" tragically died on the cusp of a second Renaissance. The Order of the Grand Pattern that Van Horowitz founded split into a hundred sub-orders, exploring in a new (and more integrated) way the fields that science once pursued. Huge advances were made in the fields of psychology and psychiatry, for instance, and a whole slew of medication-free treatment regiments were discovered. Autism and schizophrenia, once thought to be biochemical, were finally identified for what they were: a side-effect of an incomplete perception of the Landscape, a cognitive shift brought about from seeing what others didn't. Neither were cured, but the new treatments rendered them relatively mild and manageable. Depression rates declined by eighty percent, and symptom clusters once thought to be a single mental disorder were found to be two, or ten, or a spectrum. Accompanying advances in neurology aided treatment of those cases that did require medication.

Quantum mechanics saw similar advances as well, most notably the discovery of Fundamental Fields. The old notion wave-particle duality, once itself thought fundamental, was actually a threshold effect of these strange[12] new fields. Stellar

[12] As the force-transmitting Vonons of fundamental fields were of a different scale than Bosons and Fermions, they obeyed different mathematical-

evolutionary theory made it possible to identify the properties of whole star systems based only on the properties of the light of their suns. Hundreds of new materials were discovered as well; most were a mere curiosity, or too expensive to produce in scale, but metaceramics soon replaced the plastic of old, while also being largely recyclable.

Everyday life outside of the Order was only indirectly affected for most, beyond the added convenience of metaceramics. Yet a renewed sense of purpose infused it, and a new peace. Materialism declined commensurate with material wealth. The fear, deep-seated, that man had fallen short of his inborn destiny dissipated. Beyond tiny variations, the world could not but be as it was.[13] Interpreting the GP breathed new life into philosophy as well, reviving everything from Neoplatonism and Scholasticism to Chinese Folk Religion.

Now, it cannot be denied that, by the standards of our forbearers, modern civilization has failed. Families are poorer; capitalism has essentially collapsed into mercantilism and communalism[14]; old cities were abandoned for a hundred sound reasons; space programs and particle accelerators and pocket computers are nothing but museum pieces. But such people would inevitably have to ask themselves—and they often did—what was the point of all these endeavors, if not to gain a deeper understanding of the world and increase the well-being of mankind? On those fronts, we have succeeded beyond their wildest dreams. The cultural, philosophical, metaphysical, and emotional advances of the New Renaissance have breathed new life into global civilization, and the fact that we enjoy these things on horseback or by candlelight shouldn't be seen as a failure on our part. They were rather barking up the wrong tree.

In retrospect, the End of Growth was the beginning of peace, and the Death of Knowledge was the birth of wisdom. And if the people of bygone eras were unable to see the worth of our "limited" world, then theirs is simply a failure of imagination.

---

physical laws; as this was beyond direct observation, it never would have been uncovered by science, and at best may have been stumbled upon by daydreaming and blind luck.

[13] The laws and constant-sets that gave rise to man in the first place likewise limited his field of action.

[14] "Collapsed" by their standards; the Order is well-aware that most prefer our current systems.

THE NECROMANCY LINE

BY KIRSTEN CROSS

"The dead are coming! Stand to! Stand to, you ugly bastards! Stand to!"

The nightly call went out and the navvies excavating the latest tunnel underneath the streets of London stopped digging, removed their caps and turned their backs to the rails. In silence they waited for the Necromancy Line to steam past on its nightly journey on to one of London's seven main cemeteries and deliver another cargo of the city's dead.

It didn't do to watch the train pass. It didn't do at all. A man could be lost in a heartbeat if he turned and saw the ghost train thunder past.

The Necromancy Line was the line of the dammed - not something that should be witnessed by the living. It was a wise man who kept his countenance to himself until the train had steamed its way into the blackness of the tunnel and on to the burial plots of the city's 'gardens of the dead'. So despite its regular nightly journeys from the mortuaries in the city through the expanding network of underground railway tunnels and on to the cemeteries in the north and west, very few of the living ever saw the Necromancy Line pass.

The men tensed as they heard the rhythmic approach of the train, its engine chuffing like a snorting bull, ready to impale anyone who stepped in front of its V-shaped scoop. Clouds of thick, soot-incrusted smoke billowed ahead and filled the tunnel, and a hissing like a thousand snakes being driven en masse through the narrow, brick-lined passage made the men's blood run cold.

All kinds of rumours and stories surrounded the Necromancy Line.

It was driven by Death himself.

The cogs and pistons were made from the bones of children.

The boiler was hardened human skin that had been riveted into place with teeth extracted from bloated corpses.

The scream of the whistle was the scream of the dead, crying out for mercy and raging against their fate: to rot in a grave, to become nothing more than food for the worms and maggots.

The fire was started with a spark from Hell itself, and the stokers were murderers, rapists and child killers.

Children who had suffered the slow, agonising descent into pulmonary failure gathered and guarded the bodies of the deceased. These TB victims were the angry dead. The ones for whom all the scientific and medical advances of the age of Steam had been for nothing. The ones who lay choking and gasping as the disease's grip tightened around their frail chests and squeezed the last breath of life from their lungs. It was a cruel and vile death, so the spirits of TB victims were restless and violent, refusing to disembark from the Necromancy Line and journey on to their final rest. They clung to the outside of the carriages like leeches, howling and snatching at the living as they thundered past. Anyone who turned and faced them would be scooped up—kicking, screaming and begging for mercy—to tend to the cargo of putrefying bodies as conductors. There was no use crying and pleading. The children never showed any mercy, no matter how innocent the victim. After all, TB showed no mercy, so why should its victims?

The team of men bowed their heads as the scream of the train's whistle echoed through the corridors, tunnels and brick-lined passageways of the new underground system. London was in the midst of a revolution that would bring the Empire greater wealth, fame and notoriety than ever before. But no matter what advancements were made, Death was still relentless. It took every Londoner eventually, no matter how great or good, how low or wicked. The automaton experts of Clerkenwell may have been masters at replacing broken limbs, the rubies and diamonds that balanced the hair-fine cogs of their creations acquired from the gem dealers of Hatton Garden, and the tiny metal cogs crafted by the artisans of Islington. But while limbs could be replaced with extraordinarily delicate prosthetics driven by miniature steam pumps, the essence that gave every soul life, every man, woman and child a purpose and that spark of humanity; that was something that could never be replaced by cogs and gears. In the age of Steam, humanity was still an incredibly fragile blossom in the midst of a dark, metallic and soot-encrusted world.

The train's whistle screamed again. The men shuddered. They could hear a chorus of voices in that note, and not simply the tinny, metallic hoot of a whistle crafted by a living engineer. This was a scream that told of the terrors of Purgatory, that left no doubt that Death was not merely the end of life, but the beginning of an eternity of suffering. The roar of the furnace fuelled by Hellfire itself boomed and crackled, a stinging sulphurous stench sending out fingers of caustic gas that curled into the men's nostrils and made them choke.

But still they didn't turn around.

A third and final time the train's whistle screeched, and this time the cries of the dead were clearly audible in the crescendo of sound that bounced around the tunnel. This was the final warning for the living to turn away and shield their eyes from the train's passing. A final chance to avoid being snatched from the safety of the living world and carried away into the darkness of Hell itself. The roar of the engine filled every inch of the tunnel, far louder than the normal trains that rattled through during the day. This was a sound full of fury. Full of anger. Full of rage. The dead were certainly not going peacefully into that good night...

Jimmy O'Doughty was only fifteen. He'd fled the horror stories of starvation and suffering that his parents and grandparents had endured during the Great Famine. Even now, some twenty years later, life in rural Ireland was appallingly hard, and Jimmy had also grown up on tales of how there was a better life to be had beyond the borders of Fermanagh and in the gold-paved streets of London. So he'd saved up for an airship ticket and followed his brothers across the sea to England, earning a pittance working as a tipper in the tunnels of the newly emerging London Underground system.

He'd quickly discovered that the streets were certainly not paved with gold, and that despite the extraordinary juxtaposition between the poverty of rural Ireland and the wealth of the heart of the British Empire, there was still plenty of room in London for an underclass of poverty-stricken workers. These workers gravitated towards the hard manual labour of the tunnels. They rarely saw the light of day. They rarely saw their thirtieth birthday, too.

The older men were hard on young lads like Jimmy, and were liberal in dishing out a kick or two to their britches if they thought the youngsters were slacking. Jimmy's backside was still sore from the well-aimed hobnailed kick Sean Flannigan had delivered earlier; administered not because Jimmy had been slacking but because Sean had had a gin-soaked row with a tuppenny whore the night before and was still in a foul mood. Jimmy had felt the full force of that wrath, and knew he wouldn't be able to sit on that side of his backside for at least a couple of days.

He shuddered and hunched his shoulders. This was his first experience of the Necromancy Line. He'd heard stories, of course. Everyone had. But the reality was something else. It was tangible. It had a smell, a sound, a taste in the back of the throat that blended sulphur and a stinking miasma of putrid odours, making Jimmy gag. This ghost train was not mist and mystery. It was preceded by a pulse of air that damn near pushed him sideways, toppling him towards the tracks and under those clattering wheels. Jimmy leaned against the thickening air and braced his knees, fighting the urge to stagger and trip.

A rough hand grabbed his collar and steadied him. Sean Flannigan glanced down at the boy and scowled. "Hold steady, boy. Hold steady!" He kept a tight grip on the lad, pulling him closer so that the skinny little lad could brace himself against Flannigan's massive muscular bulk. He might have chastised the lad for slacking off earlier, but he didn't want to see the poor little bogtrotter end up under the wheels of the Necromancy Line. Nobody deserved that fate...

The roar became deafening and the train burst out of the blackness and into the tunnel section. Gaslights guttered and spluttered, the flames blasted sideways by the change in air pressure. The wheels screeched and screamed their way along the metal rails. The roar was supplemented by a cacophony of wailing voices, all begging the huddled men to turn around and witness their plight. The men hunched their shoulders harder, buried their heads into their chests and screwed their eyes tight shut.

Don't look.

Don't look.

Don't look...

The men felt a blast of savage heat as the engine thundered past. On the footplate sweating, emaciated figures struggled with shovels, relentlessly filling the furnace with fuel. Their eyes had been replaced with glowing coals from the firebox itself, so that they could carry out their duty without succumbing to the deathly gaze of the engine Driver. These were the murderers who would not repent. The rapists who took pleasure in the suffering of others. The sadists, monsters and beasts that had spent their lives hounding, abusing and violating the innocent. Their fate was to ride the Necromancy Line for eternity, stoking its boiler and feeling the fires of Hell slowly burning their skin and their souls into ashes.

At the front of the engine was a shadow that no earthly light could penetrate. Here stood the Driver. A Steam-age ferryman taking the dead across the River Fleet, rather than the Styx. A figure whom no creature could look upon and live. Whom no man could bear the touch of, and who would carry out his duty without fear or favour. His was the ultimate job; to take the dead from this world and into the next. He did not judge. He did not offer mercy, countenance or hope. He merely drove the engine. Bony fingers reached up and he tugged at the whistle again, announcing the arrival of the Necromancy Line. Any who turned to witness its passing were doomed.

Next came the carriages. Liveried in black and red, they had the outward appearance of normal Pullmans; the kind that would regularly ferry the gentry of London from the leafy suburbs of Battersea or Camden and into the heart of the city. But these were not populated by well-dressed ladies and gentlemen heading to the opera or to the boutiques of Bond Street. These were filled with regimented corpses, each one languishing in a coffin or wrapped in a shroud, and attended on by hollow-eyed wraiths that moaned and wailed.

Even on the Necromancy Line, there were class divisions. In First Class the coffins were more ornate. Deep red curtains trimmed with gold brocade swayed at the windows, held in place by matching gold braids and finished with tassels that jiggled and splayed, agitated by the motion of the train. Here, the moans and wails were more respectful. These were the corpses of the wealthy—those who could afford to pay the driver more than the usual two pennies. Two half-sovereigns covering the eyes would grant you passage in style. However, even the rich were not guaranteed a favourable reception at the end of the line, no matter how much they were prepared to pay the Driver.

In the Third Class carriages the bodies were lucky if they were stuffed unceremoniously into a pine box, and some merely had linen shrouds covering their rigamortis-stiffened bodies. There were no red velvet curtains, no gold brocade. No spectral mourners to mark their passing. Just the cold, hard floor and a carriage filled with the stench of death. Shining half-sovereigns were replaced by grubby pennies.

Outside the carriages clung the souls of the restless dead. Their fingers embedded deep into the metal skin of the Pullmans, they had refused to let go at journey's end. So their job, until they chose to move on to the next phase, was to snatch and grab at the backs of the living, trying to lure another soul aboard to act as a conductor. Those who succumbed were doomed to wander the carriages, collect the coins and issue tickets—not quite dead but no longer living. It promised nothing but a slow, lingering decay that took lifetime upon lifetime. Eventually, when the Driver offered release, those who had been press-ganged into service willingly took his hand.

Jimmy felt bony fingers brush the back of his neck. Small hands grasped and tugged on the back of his jacket. He stumbled as one particularly hard pull nearly tugged him off his feet.

Sean Flannigan pulled the lad closer. Damn those foul little monsters! They always went for the youngsters. The smaller they were, the frailer of countenance, the more those blasted souls seemed to want them for their own. *'Well, not this time, you evil bastards! Not this time!'* Sean grabbed the lad by his shoulders and pushed him in front of him, putting his massive bulk between the grasping hands of the damned and Jimmy's little body. "Eyes front, boy!" he howled above the roar of the train. "Keep your eyes front!" He gave the lad a hard shake to drive home the point. In the lea of Sean Flannigan's body, Jimmy was protected from the grabbing hands and clawing fingers of the dead. The terrified boy covered his ears with his hands and grimaced, trying desperately not to weep with fear.

Sean, however, was enduring everything that the relentless demons clinging to the outside of the train could throw at him. Now they were really angry. He'd taken their prize from them! Fingers that were nothing more than bone with ribbons of rotting flesh hanging from the tips swiped and clawed at his back. His thin shirt quickly turned from a perfectly serviceable cotton garment into ragged tatters fit for nothing more than the rubbish heap. Underneath the torn shirt his body fared no better. He flinched as he felt nails slash into his back, slicing deep through skin and into muscle. His blood ran freely, sending the howling fiends into a frenzy. They knew that they were close to making the big man falter. But they only had seconds to make him succumb and turn. Then? Oh, *then*, he would be theirs...

Time thickened and slowed. The furious pounding of the pistons seemed to fluctuate, and the roar of the engine faded and muted. The train slowed to a crawl, the movement of the pistons blurring and smearing their way through a distortion in Time that only the dead could see. The Driver sensed the change in the atmosphere and casually looked back to where his passengers were fixated on the bloody, wavering figure of Sean Flannigan. The big man still stood resolutely with his back turned to the train, trying not to cry out in pain as another hand with fingers like bony daggers slashed into his skin. The Driver watched impassively. They needed new conductors for both the First and the Third Class carriages. The hulking navvy would make the perfect candidate. Of course, whether he took that role was up to him. If he turned, he would join the Necromancy Line. If he didn't, he would survive to see another day.

All it would take would be one sideways glance at his tormentors, and Sean Flannigan would be doomed to an eternity of servitude, damnation and a lingering, living death. He crumpled to his knees and cried out, calling for his Ma, for God, for the holy guardian Angels, damn it, for *anything* to help him resist the torment. He couldn't hold out much longer.

Jimmy felt the big man behind him drop down.

Without thinking, he turned...

The damned let out a howl of joy and Jimmy felt himself being lifted off his feet and dragged by clawing, grasping hands towards the train. Now he had looked, he couldn't turn away. The ghostly forms that swarmed around the train's sides were faded and white, almost translucent. Black sockets and gaping maws contorted angelic faces into snarling grimaces, the fury at their fate etched into every line. Some were just children. Others were older, but the ravages of disease and poverty had emaciated their bodies to such an extent that it was difficult to tell how old they had really been at the point of death.

Jimmy screamed in utter terror, a long, wailing agonising cry that tore at the heart of the men. They knew his fate. But if they turned, they'd suffer the same. Better to let the Driver and his passengers have the young lad and spare them.

But Sean Flannigan wasn't prepared to let the lad suffer for his weakness. So he turned too, and stared up the line towards the engine where the Driver stood silently watching Jimmy's struggles. Sean looked straight at the blackness that surrounded the Driver. He pulled himself up to his full height and balled his fists, ignoring the slashing, grasping hands of the passengers. His face contorted into a snarl. "Take me instead, damn you! He's just a boy. You bastards wanted me? Then take me! Here I am, come on, what are you waiting for? Spare the lad! *Spare him!"*

The darkness shimmered and started to congeal into an almost-solid form. Pinpricks of blue-white light glowed in the centre of a cowl-shaped outline, like two stars in the blackness of empty space. Part of the darkness formed into an arm and a long, skeletal finger pointed at Sean.

The words, when they came, filled the tunnel in a whisper that passed through solid flesh and spoke directly to the soul of every man. *"Take them both."* There was no mercy. No remorse. Both men had turned. So both men would be taken.

"NO!" Sean Flannigan raged at the Driver and started to run towards him. "No, you bastard, *no!* Spare the boy!" Sean pounded past First Class and towards the engine footplate. He reached out to grab at the Driver.

The two pinpricks of blue-white light focused their attention on the grasping, shouting man. A strong man. A defiant man. He would make a good conductor. The Driver flicked a spectral finger and Sean Flannigan was lifted off his feet and thrown backwards through the air. As his arms and legs flailed he felt dozens of hands grabbing him and pulling him towards an open carriage window. He twisted his head and looked back, just in time to seek poor little Jimmy being hauled into Third Class. The desperate wail of the lad as he disappeared was the last thing that Sean Flannigan ever heard in this world.

The Driver turned back to the engine's levers and turned a huge handle. The knuckle of the handle protested briefly and then relented. He tapped a gauge, watched the needle dance its way up and around the numbers. When he was satisfied that the pressure was at the right level, he released a lever. Jets of super-heated steam blasted out from either side of the engine wheels and the pistons shuddered back into life. They pumped furiously and the wheels spun on the track, frantically trying to gain traction on the slippery rails. The pistons went into hard reverse and then forward again. Finally, the wheels gained purchase and the train started to move.

The remaining men stayed hunched and shaking, resolutely refusing to turn and meet the same fate as Sean and the lad. Sean would be a big loss to the team. His strength and skill as a navvy had made him invaluable. The lad—well, a loss, for sure. But men died all the time in the tunnels. A letter of condolence would be sent to his family, along with a few shilling's pay (once money for his lodgings and food had been docked), and a family back in Ireland would bury an empty coffin and grieve at the side of an empty grave.

Sean's family would get a little more, but they too would bury an empty coffin.

The train, complete with not one but two new conductors, restarted its journey back down the line and towards the first of the cemetery stops for tonight. The wails faded until finally silence flooded back into the tunnel.

The remaining men crossed themselves several times, thanking whatever guardian Angel had watched over them that they were spared. Slowly, reluctantly, they turned back to the line to pick up where they'd left off. A cracked rail needed to be lifted and replaced. Three fractured stakes had to be prized out of the ground and new ones put in.

As they stepped back onto the line the men stopped, their attention caught by the glint of something shining amongst the stones. One gruff-voiced man pointed at the object. "Flynn, what's that, then?"

"What?"

"That!" The man pointed again.

"Where, Robbie?"

"Right there, you blind bugger! In front of you!"

Flynn looked down and frowned. "Looks like a locket." He bent down and scooped up the object in his huge, battered and blackened hands. Nestled in the palm of his hand was a small silver locket. Carefully prizing the two halves of the locket open with a grubby fingernail, he beckoned to Robbie. "Bring that light over here, man, I can't see a damned thing!"

Robbie grumbled and muttered, pushing his way through the crowd of men. He held up the lamp, casting a yellow pool of light on Flynn's hand. The men clustered closer, all curious to see what keepsake lay in the heart of the locket.

On the left was a tiny photo of a stern-looking woman. Black hair was pulled back into a tight bun, and a plain and slightly dowdy skirt bolstered by several layers of petticoats flared out from her waist. She was in profile with her face turned slightly towards the right.

She looked lost. Sad. Haunted.

On the other side and pressed behind a piece of glass was a single lock of hair. Flynn turned the locket over and squinted at the inscription on the back. He wasn't good at reading, but he had enough education to be able to spell out the words.

To my boy Jimmy. God keep you safe always. Your loving Ma.

Flynn snapped the locket shut and tried to ignore the stinging sensation in his eye as a hot tear threatened to break free.

The poor lad had only been fifteen. *Fifteen,* damn it!

But the Necromancy Line had taken him and Sean anyway.

Flynn closed his enormous fist around the locket and glowered into the darkness. Further down the line, more teams of men would be turning their backs as they heard the three whistles of the Necromancy Line. They too would be praying that they wouldn't feel the grabbing hands of the dead, and would fight the urge to turn and watch the train as it screamed past.

Men would be screwing their eyes shut and trying not to think of the horrors that thundered past them, only inches away. They had free will. They could choose to keep their back to the train as it passed, no matter what the spectral demons tried to do. Or they could turn. Their choice would determine whether they survived to see another day, or became part of the train's company.

The Driver didn't make that decision for them. He never judged. He never granted mercy. He never wavered.

And now two new conductors wandered the carriages, taking payment from the eyes of the dead.

EAR WORM

BY RAMON ROZAS III

"Well, here we are," I said, smoothing down my tie. "Let's go talk to the President."

"Senator," Wu corrected. She was perfectly composed in the little ante-room of the Blair House. "He's not president until tomorrow." She held up a black, heavily encrypted USB drive. "Want me to handle this?"

"Yes," I said, opening the door to the House conference room. I strode through it with a confidence I didn't feel, and Wu followed me.

Sitting in the plush audience chairs were the Senator and his soon-to-be White House Chief of Staff, Jeff Gazer. In the back loitered a trim, dark-suited man with an earpiece. He was Secret Service, and I knew he was cleared for this briefing.

"Good evening, Senator," I said with forced cheerfulness as I took my place at the podium already set up in the room. There was a big LED screen behind me for presentations. Wu slid behind me and quickly plugged the drive into its slot in the wall.

"Good evening, Mister....," the Senator trailed off meaningfully.

His aide was not nearly so polite. "Who the hell are you, and why the hell did you demand a meeting at 9:00 p.m. before the inauguration?" Gazer barked. "If the last Chief of Staff hadn't basically black-mailed me to schedule this, we'd be going over budget projections."

"And if the outgoing President hadn't asked me to go along with it," the Senator added, "you would not be here."

"Fair enough, sir. Please give me ten minutes of your time and I think you'll see how important this meeting is." I tapped my phone and pulled up the first slide on the big screen.

"My name is Zachariah Spears, and this is my assistant Capt. Adeline Wu, on loan from the Army." Wu nodded, looking military even in her civilian pencil skirt and jacket. "

"I am the director of the division of the National Security Agency in charge of Project TREBLE MOIRA." I cleared my throat. "While not public knowledge, I am the person actually in charge of the mass collection of voice mails, texts, emails and other internet information under intelligence programs PRISM, CARNIVORE, BULLRUN and MAINWAY, among others."

Gazer snorted. "Goddammit, man, is that what this is about? What the—"

The Senator held up a hand, and Gazer cut off his comment. The politician looked hard at me. "I campaigned against all of those programs. Hell, I filibustered some of them in the Senate before I even ran for President."

"Yes sir, you did."

Silence for a moment. "I'm guessing you didn't vote for me, eh?"

I decided on the truth. "No sir, I voted for your opponent. Mostly because she was a Cabinet member in the prior administration and thus was already cleared for TREBLE MOIRA." I gave a nervous laugh. "Therefore I could avoid this briefing."

"I assume you are here to tell me of the 'grave danger to national security' if I cancel these projects and shutter your division, right?" the Senator had a mocking half-smile on his face. "Your boss at the NSA tried it on me once before, during the budget vote last year." He shook his head. "It didn't work. Why do you think you'll do better?"

"My boss never told you the whole truth, because you weren't TREBLE MOIRA cleared as a junior senator, sir. Screw 'dangers to national security'; I'm here to tell you exactly what my division does, and why closing it would be *an existential threat to the human species.*"

The Senator's eyebrows raised along with my voice. "Okay. You have the ten minutes I promised the president."

"Thank you." I took a deep breath and clicked to the next slide, which was a grainy photo of poor damned Larson and his team of researchers.

"This is Doctor Harvey Larson of Stanford and his team. In the 1960's, he did tremendous – groundbreaking, in fact – work on sonic weapons, and their psychological effect. His team came up with The Curdler, a sonic weapon later used on several runs in Vietnam as part of Project Wandering Soul. The device sent out ultrafrequency vibrations which spooked Viet Cong snipers, and sent them running."

Next slide. "The Larson team was sure they could come up with something more effective than that, and, unfortunately, they did." This slide was a black-and-white vid, showing a dingy concrete-block room with a test subject inside of it, and a large glass window on one side. The man had big bulky vintage headphones on, and was sitting at a metal table. A date stamp in the corner read "03/13/68."

I started the video, and through the window could be seen the control room, where a technician started a tape machine. By habit, I double-checked the sound – there was none.

The man on the screen sat normally for a few seconds, then sat bolt upright. His eyes fixed on the concrete wall in a thousand-yard stare. It was hard to see with the bad quality of the late-sixties recording equipment, but looking closely you could see he was trembling as every muscle in his body shook. A bloody froth began to run from his mouth.

I had watched this video hundreds of times—maybe thousands—and I still winced at what happened next. Two uniformed orderlies entered the frame from what I knew was an off-screen door and grabbed the subject.

He went berserk, clawing and biting at the orderlies like a mad animal. In the fray, his headphones fell off.

The operators hadn't turned the sound off.

Within seconds the two orderlies were jerking on the floor, drool dripping from their mouths. The first subject, loping like a wild animal, ran off-screen and (I knew from history) out of the door.

I stopped the video. "That containment breach cost Dr. Larson and most of his team their lives."

The Senator was shocked. "What the hell was that?"

"The Larson team had inadvertently discovered TREBLE MOIRA, although at the office we call it 'Hell's Bells.'" I smiled tightly at the joke. "It is a series of tonal sounds, a tune really, which upon hearing causes complete destruction of the listener's higher brain functions and turns them into raving madmen. *Homicidal* raving madmen." I tapped to the next slide.

Dead sheep were scattered across a valley—thousands of them. "It gets worse. Turns out that contaminated individuals have an uncontrollable compulsion to whistle, sing and hum TREBLE MOIRA—which spreads it to other subjects." I gestured at the screen. "The Larson experiments were at Dugway Proving Ground in Utah. Contaminated individuals spread through the base and then into the surrounding countryside. 6400 sheep were killed, confirming that TREBLE MOIRA can affect other mammals. Luckily, subsequent testing shows they can't seem to spread it themselves."

"Wait a minute, I've heard of that," Gazer said suddenly. "That wasn't some weird song, it was a nerve gas leak. Thousands of sheep dropped dead. The Army paid millions in compensation."

"That was the cover story. We—and by 'we' I mean the Army, the CIA and assorted other agencies—had to spread VX nerve agent on all of those sheep carcasses, inject it into the Pecks—a local family—and make sure plenty of clues pointed to that. The truth was way too dangerous to let out. Fortunately—or unfortunately—Larson's team left meticulous notes, and the Army was able to recreate TREBLE MOIRA and experiment on it further." I tapped the next slide.

The next scene was an old satellite photo. "Sverdlovsk, Soviet Union—1979. A supposed anthrax leak from a weapons factory kills more than 100 people. The Soviets deny anything." The next slide came up—a corpse wearing rough cloth clothes and lying half-frozen on a snowbank. Male, its eyes were frozen with a wild look and bloody froth framed its mouth.

"The CIA was able to obtain brain tissue samples from some of the victims. They showed the classic signs of exposure to TREBLE MOIRA. This was our first real confirmation that the Soviets had obtained TREBLE MOIRA, probably through espionage."

The next slide was a desert terrain. "Lop Nur, China—1986. An alleged outbreak—"

"Mr. Spears!" the Senator interrupted. "Even if I believe all of this, what the devil does this have to do with domestic spying?"

"TREBLE MOIRA is essentially a song, sir. And what happens to music in the 21st century?" I tapped forward to slide 18.

Two words blazed on the screen. FILE SHARING.

My mouth was dry, but there was no water on the podium. I swallowed hard. "In December 1999, the U.S. Army and the CIA were jointly alerted by A&M Records to certain MP3 files that were being hosted on a file-sharing service called Napster. You all remember Napster?"

The room was silent.

"You could upload any song you owned, and download any song any other member had uploaded. The birth of music piracy. As you can imagine, the record labels were very keen on investigating Napster. However, we got called because their investigators kept downloading this one file and then throwing themselves out of their office windows."

I grimaced. "You can guess what happened. Someone, somewhere, somehow had uploaded TREBLE MOIRA to Napster and it was being downloaded, copied and spread everywhere."

I looked at them in the audience. The senator and his aide were staring at me with growing horror in their eyes.

I shook my head. "Ever since then, the NSA—with help from the recording industry—has been trying desperately to make sure that TREBLE MOIRA does not get released into the general population. We create honey pot piracy sites to keep people in controlled environments –"

Wu spoke up. "The guys in Sweden are ours."

"—and we work with manufacturers to make sure devices won't play unsanctioned music files. We scan petabytes and petabytes of data *every second* looking for any sign that someone has shared, downloaded or played TREBLE MOIRA. An uncontrollable outbreak in a major urban area would be—well, catastrophic."

The Senator rubbed his face with his hands. "And other presidents knew about this."

"If you recall, your predecessor—the current president for a few more hours—also campaigned on eliminating the mass surveillance programs. He *expanded* them after learning about TREBLE MOIRA."

"You're talking about—shit, you've got an audible zombie virus here!"

I nodded. "That comparison has been made before, sir. And by that analogy, we're the CDC."

I looked at the clock on the wall. "And that's my time, Mr.—senator. If you have any questions, I will be available at your convenience during the transition."

"Just hearing it can drive you crazy?"

"Or seeing the notation, if you can read music. Yes, we found that out the hard way."

"Be straight with me—how bad is it?"

I looked right into his eyes. "I wasn't joking about the extinction of humanity, sir."

Wu and I took our hard drive and left.

In the Agency limo back to the NSA offices, I opened a bottle of scotch and shakily poured both of us two fingers. "What do you think?"

"You did good, sir." She sipped her drink, staring out at the lights.

"Did he get it?"

"I think so." She kept watching the famous monuments and buildings slide past on our way to Fort Meade.

"So why are you so concerned, Wu?"

"If he didn't get it, sir. What do we do next?"

"He jogs every morning." I knocked back the rest of my scotch. "We see if we can get access to his mp3 player," I said.

SOULS OF LIT

BY JEAN GRAHAM

This morning, Mary Queen of Scots and the Count of Monte Cristo would both be dropping in for tea.

The gray Cornish sky threatened rain. Undaunted, Winton Coles wound his way down Darley's sloping high street and turned into the short, brick-paved lane of Abbey Mews. In this cul-de-sac that had once, in centuries past, led to an abbey carriage house and stable, there were very few shops: Batterton's Coins and Stamps, Lorena's China Niche, his own Mews Bookshop, and two unoccupied spaces that had sported TO LET signs for the better part of two years.

As he had done every morning for thirty-three of his fifty-two years, Winton unlocked the Mews Bookshop's glass multi-paned door, eased it open and stepped in to greet his myriad ghostly friends. The fact that none of them was living (and some had never lived at all) bothered Winton not a whit.

The antique brass sheep's bell had jangled overhead when he'd opened the door, and the delightful scents of aged leather, old cloth and old paper had assailed him, all comfortable familiarities that were as much a part of Winton as breath, bone and blood.

"Good morning," he said. The shop's ceiling-high shelves, filled with volumes of every conceivable size, shape and genre, declined, for the moment, to answer. All of the books were perfectly, painstakingly alphabetized by author's surname (except for the non-fiction, organized instead by subject), and each cover page bore the crisp mark of a price that had been inscribed with a number three pencil in Winton's neat, precise hand.

The incandescent lights buzzed to life overhead and hummed a soft, one-note symphony in the key of G. On his way to the sales counter, Winton nodded a collective good morning to Jane Austen, Charles Dickens, Samuel Clemens, Rudyard Kipling, Thomas Hardy, Mary Shelley, Herman Melville, John Milton, Sir Walter Scott and Robert Louis Stevenson – among others. In the math and technology section, he also smiled and greeted a tiny, eight-legged denizen who perched in an intricate, miniature web stretching a mere six centimeters between book and bookshelf. This was the only spider he'd ever declined to evict from the store, and that solely because it had perspicaciously constructed its home atop a volume entitled *Integrated System Networks.* Winton still couldn't help chuckling every time he passed the spot.

Behind the counter, he switched on both the radio and the small electric hot plate nestled (at a safe distance) between piles of unsorted books. While Sir Neville Mariner conducted Mozart's 40th from St. Martin-in-the-Fields in London, he filled a dented copper kettle with water from the porcelain-tapped sink, and presently, his tea tray rattling with three cups, three saucers and a pot of hot, steeping tea, Winton made his way around the counter and in between towering shelves to the haven.

He'd always called it the haven. Stella had always insisted that "reading room" was more appropriate, but to Winton, it was far more than a mere place in which to read. The central "room," formed by surrounding bookshelf "walls," harbored an overstuffed Victorian sofa, reading lamps, a thick Persian rug and a massive oak library table ringed with comfortable chairs, all of it a rather tight fit in the limited space – but Winton's guests had never once complained.

Two books lay, closed, upon the table. Winton placed his tray next to these, pulled up his favorite reading chair, and with Beethoven's Moonlight Sonata serenading from the nearby counter, pulled the two waiting volumes toward him.

A History of England opened readily to the well-thumbed sixteenth century. Alexandre Dumas' *The Count of Monte Cristo* he opened to the title page, prepared to delve into its wonders from the beginning – for the fifth (or was it the sixth?) time. He read the first three pages in silence while the tea steeped and the antique French clock nestled in the travel section ticked quietly to itself.

Her Majesty arrived first. She emerged, rather appropriately, Winton thought, from the history shelf and proceeded to fold herself into the armchair opposite Winton. She wore a gathered blue silk gown that had been trimmed with white fur, and she favored him with an enigmatic smile. Winton returned the latter, poured each of them a steaming cup of tea, and said, "A very good morning to you, Your Majesty."

"Good morrow to you as well, good sir. And how fareth the keeper of our royal library?" inquired the queen, whose Elizabethan parlance, it seemed, still needed a bit of work.

"Passing fair," Winton replied. "Though I won't deny that things have been better."

"Ah." Queen Mary, who wore the late Mrs. Esther Pangborne's face, reached out to caress Winton's hand.

She couldn't really touch him, of course, but the gesture was a sympathetic display of support that he appreciated anyway. "Your sister Stella again, is it?"

Winton nodded. He hadn't really intended to mention Stella. He'd come today prepared to discuss the inner workings of the sixteenth century Scottish court, the queen's legendary tryst with David Rizzio, the birth of James – anything other than Stella and her impossible plans for the bookstore. Somehow, though, he found no inspiration in their usual intellectual pursuits this morning.

"Stella wants to close the shop," he said miserably, "or at the very least, get rid of all the books. Some piffle or other about turning it into a pizza parlor, because that's the sort of business that could bring in oh-so-many more tourists, and more importantly, many, many more pounds. Can you believe that?"

Queen Mary's already-furrowed brow wrinkled further. (Winton had never seen fit to point out that Mrs. Pangborne's age at the point of her death had far exceeded Mary Stuart's when the monarch's unfortunate neck had met with the executioner's axe. It was one of Esther's favorite roles, and who was he to discourage her?)

"Tourists?" the indignant queen echoed. "A *pizza parlor?* Why that's... that's... well it's simply unthinkable, that's what it is! How could she do such a thing?"

"84 Charing Cross Road," Winton mumbled, referring to Helene Hanff's splendid biography about her long-standing correspondence with the famous London book seller. "It's an American pizza franchise now, did you know that? Imagine. After all those many years filled to the rafters with beautiful, antiquarian, hard-to-find books, only to meet the ignominious end of being turned into a pizza house. It's a blatant crime against literary humanity."

"Quite blatant," the queen echoed. "A pity there wasn't a law..."

"Well, she shan't be getting rid of us," said a bass voice. Winton looked up in time to see Edmond Dantès step forth from the first editions shelf to take a chair beside the queen. Dumas' hero wore the earthly visage of Alfred Glover, who until recently had been one of Winton's best customers. The Mews Bookshop had purchased back most of Alfred's library upon his death, but apparently not content to leave these particular worldly goods behind, Alfred had been returning to visit his books ever since. As had Esther Pangborne and Gerald Fenton and a number of other former owners of Winton's rather vast literary inventory.

"I've really no idea what to do," Winton said dismally. "Legally speaking, you see, it's *Stella's* bookshop. As the elder sibling, it was she who inherited the business and, sad to say, the deed to the store." He poured the count a cup of tea. "She says it's losing far too much money these days, and that the drain will send her to an early grave if we don't shut it down."

"Losing money my foot!" Mary declared in a somewhat less-than-queenly manner. "How can it possibly lose money? If she holds the deed, there is no rent to pay, surely?"

"Ah, but there *could* be, couldn't there?" Dantès stroked his beard, contemplating. "Rent paid to *her* if she removes the books and acquires a paying tenant with another sort of shop to run. A *profitable* shop. Do I have it right?"

"I'm afraid so." Winton sighed. "I won't deny that I've bought many more books than I've sold of late. And Stella's right about one other thing. The tourists almost never buy books anymore. All they seem to want these days are those dreadful DVDs, CDs, computer games, and oh yes – a great deal of pizza."

"Well, it simply cannot be permitted," the queen decreed. Then, letting her royal persona slip altogether, Esther Pangborne declared, "Besides, I haven't had the chance to play *half* the parts I want to play yet. There's still Mary Magdalene, Guenevere, Madame Curie, Eleanor of Aquitaine..."

"Yes, yes, dear, I'm sure," Edmond Dantès interrupted. "But all of that aside, surely there is *something* we can do to prevent this disaster?"

"I'm open to suggestions." With another lengthy sigh, Winton sipped at his tea, barely conscious of Rachmaninov's Vespers whispering from the radio in the background. Rain had begun pattering on the roof overhead. And that, Winton knew only too well, would serve to discourage tourist and resident customers alike (as though either needed more discouraging these days).

Midway through Winton's second cup of tea, the shop's bell rang.

"Well, well," he muttered. "It sounds as though someone has braved the wet to visit us."

But the "someone," to his vast disappointment, turned out to be Stella, maneuvering her ever-broadening bulk through the narrow shop doorway and snapping shut her huge blue umbrella so that it dripped all over the threadbare carpet.

"Good morning, Stella," he said pleasantly.

She merely harrumphed at him and shuffled off toward the haven, though not without first leaning the wet umbrella against the poetry and drama shelf with its priceless first editions of Spencer and Coleridge and Bacon. Winton scurried to move it to a safer location the moment she'd passed out of sight.

When he re-entered the haven moments later, his sister had already taken up residence in Queen Mary's chair, having also commandeered Her Majesty's cup of tea. The guests, of course, had gone, vanished back into their bookshelves until such time as they might deem it safe to venture forth again. Few of the living had ever been privileged enough to see them. Stella, for one, would not likely have survived the shock.

"Never could teach you to make a decent pot of tea," she grumbled, though she drained the cup and then reached for the count's as well. "And I don't suppose you've sold any books yet today?"

Winton tried to keep any trace of resentment from showing in his eyes or voice. "It's only eleven," he said hopefully. "Give them time."

Stella sniffed. "Time! Winton, *dear heart*, this place couldn't turn a decent profit if you gave it two centuries."

"But it's been here for two centuries already," he reminded her kindly. "And nearly half of that time in the hands of our family. It's the oldest bookshop in Darley – the oldest in all of Cornwall. Can you really consider just ending all of that?"

"Oh, for heaven's sake, Winton. I wouldn't be ending it. Not exactly. I told you, I'd only be modifying the inventory a bit. All right, quite a bit, but it would be changing from a product that no longer sells to one that does! That's infinitely better than starving to death on the pittance we're bringing in now, I should think."

Quashing the uncharitable thought that Stella looked a very long way indeed from starving, Winton peered up at the shelves full of row upon row of his leather and cloth-bound treasures. "But," he implored her, "what about the books?"

Stella shrugged. "Oh, if we can't auction them off, I suppose we'll just have to box them up and store them somewhere, if we can find a place." Winton's horror at that prospect must have shown all too clearly. Stella *clanked* the empty teacup back onto its saucer with so much force, he was sure that the china must have chipped. "Winton, we've been over and *over* this! They have to go, and that's the end of it!"

Go? His life-long adventures with Joseph Conrad, Ernest Hemingway and H. Rider Haggard? His raptures at the lyrical stanzas of Emily Dickinson and Alfred Lord Tennyson? His daily tea-and-reminiscing with the role-playing spirits who shared all of his literary passions? Winton shuddered. As Her Majesty had said this morning, it was simply unthinkable.

"You can't..." Winton started to say, but at his sibling's withering glare, he retreated to employ another approach. It never paid to argue with Stella: Stella had never once in her life been wrong about anything. "It's rather like betraying your dearest friends, that's all," he reasoned. "You can't have forgotten how much you used to enjoy reading Malory, DuMaurier, all three of the Brontës? You read them aloud to me, even before I was old enough to walk. I learned all the best passages from Dickens and Lewis Carroll and L. Frank Baum, even Shakespeare, at your hand, long before I could read on my own. When we were children, you loved them all as much as I did. Don't you remember?"

The faintest glimmer of something verging on sympathy flickered in Stella's eyes, but before it could flourish, the more-familiar glint of avarice returned and promptly extinguished it. "That was a long time ago," she snapped. "Before Mum and Dad died and left me strapped with this..." She gestured angrily at the shelves. "...this bloody albatross of a bookshop!" Her gaze fell on the Dumas volume and she snatched it up to shake it in Winton's face. "No one reads these moldering old relics anymore, Winton. No one remembers them. No one buys them. No one cares!"

Somewhere in the midst of her tirade, Stella's face had turned a rather alarming shade of crimson. In all her rants and rages over all the years, Winton had never known her to go quite so red as this. Only when she began gasping for air did he realize that this was something more than a simple fit of temper. The Dumas *thumped* back to the tabletop with a bang, and the fingers that had held it began clutching wildly at empty air.

"Stella?"

Winton stumbled around the oak table's thick legs to reach her. With no idea what to do, he began pounding on her back between the shoulder blades. The tea service chattered noisily on the vibrating table.

"Stella!"

She stopped gasping. By sheer force of will, Winton tugged the chair back until he could move in front of her, hoping that his blows had dislodged whatever had been choking her. But to his dismay, he found that Stella had ceased gasping because she had also ceased breathing.

Winton slapped her cheeks, compressed her chest with both hands the way the medical books said to do it, blew air into her mouth and then pumped her chest again.

It didn't help.

The radio segued from the lengthy Vespers into a sprightly Chopin waltz.

With trembling fingers, Winton dialed the emergency number on the shop's black rotary telephone. When he returned to Stella's side, there were several figures gathered round her, all of them peering closely at her puffy, still-red face.

"Curious," Miss Marple/Esther Pangborne opined. "Most curious. No sign at all of foul play, though. Why, there's not a mark on her anywhere."

"You sure about that no foul play stuff, doll?" That wise crack came from Sam Spade/Bill Evans. "He coulda slipped her a Mickey in the tea, y'know."

"Oh, hardly." James Herriot/Milburn Hurst pretended to take poor Stella's pulse. "It's quite clearly a case of cardiac arrest. Instantaneous massive coronary. She literally never knew what hit her."

"And just how does a back roads farm vet know that?" Spade huffed. "This here's a lady, Doc, not one o' yer Yorkshire cows!"

"My dear Mr. Spade," Herriot returned indignantly, "I can assure you, a heart attack is still most certainly a heart attack, whether it should befall the lady *or* the cow!"

Sam Spade's only reply was a derisive snort.

A horrible thought had, in the meantime, occurred to Winton. "You didn't...?" he said to all of them, and then stammered the half-question again. "You didn't...?"

"Oh, dear me, of *course* not," Miss Marple averred. "We wouldn't dream of it. Not even a little bit. And anyway, she seems to have done it rather tidily all on her own, with no help from anyone else whatsoever."

"Damned peculiar timing, just the same," said Herriot. "Did anyone know she had a heart condition?"

"No," Winton told him. "But Stella always used to say this place would be the death of her." Guilt pressed him into one of the haven chairs and heavily weighted his shoulders. In fifty-two years of sharing the same house with her, he had never really been able to bring himself to like Stella. "She always said it, but I never thought..."

He left the sentence hanging while a siren began warbling in the distance, and one by one, his ghostly friends gathered round to comfort him.

Before Stella's demise, it would have been difficult for Winton to say just what had been missing. In all his years of daily get-togethers with the Mews shop's literary spirits, Winton had often enjoyed deep and stimulating conversations on an incredibly wide range of topics. But like a poorly-written novel, their gatherings had somehow lacked a certain element of... well, he could only call it *conflict*. Everyone had always made it a point to be so dreadfully, meticulously polite, the sarcastic banter that Sam Spade and company engendered notwithstanding. But true confrontation had, as a rule, been missing from their literary tete-a-tetes.

Not any longer.

Their sessions fairly sizzled nowadays, thanks to dear departed Stella's exemplary portrayals of Bloody Mary, Mrs. Danvers, Madame Defarge and a host of similarly dour, acid-tongued femme fatales. The ghosts, in various guises, emerged every morning from their respective tomes to watch

Stella's personae engage in verbal battles with the diverse likes of Albert Einstein, Ivanhoe and Ebenezer Scrooge. Margaret Sanger crossed linguistic swords with the Marquis de Sade. Madame Bovary waged a lexical war with the Sheriff of Nottingham. Lizzie Borden wielded words far sharper than her little axe against Jupiter, Napoleon, and Henry VIII.

The bookshop fairly echoed with their everyday, captivating exploits. Oh, there were, sad to say, still depressingly few customers, as well as far too little money in the bank account. But as the green grocer's bill was now only a third what it had been before Stella's crossing, Winton made do.

He had no idea how long they'd be able to keep on this way. But at least he knew one thing for a certainty.

He liked Stella *ever* so much better now.

THE PHANTOM OF THE DUST

BY JOHN MICHAEL GREER

Eighteenth-century portraits stared down from the high brown walls, and not all the faces were entirely human. Owen Merrill sat back in the brown armchair and considered them.

All around him, the great Georgian bulk of the Chaudronnier mansion murmured to itself in the night, while off beyond the curtained windows a foghorn moaned, sending faint echoes back from the soaring cliffs north of ancient Kingsport. Closer at hand, yellow light from an ornate Victorian lamp chased night to the corners of the room, spilled over Owen's sandy hair and square face, vanished into the black of his borrowed evening clothes. Dinner was long over, and most of the Chaudronnier family and their newly arrived summer guests had gone up to bed, making room at last for a conversation not suited to uninitiated ears.

Jenny Chaudronnier, who was sitting across the little table in another of the big brown chairs, refilled bone china teacups from a pot that was easily two centuries old. "So that's as much news as I've got," she said. "That, and a few bits of gossip from Miskatonic. I audited another class spring semester."

Owen turned his attention back to her, allowed a smile. "A doctorate isn't enough college for you?"

"It's a hard habit to break," she said, with an answering smile. Short, thin, and plain, with a mop of unruly mouse-colored hair, she wore a green silk evening gown that fit her figure exactly and her face and manner not at all. The Chaudronniers were one of Kingsport's ancient families, though, and clung to more than one set of customs from an earlier age.

"So what was it?"

"One of the seminars Michael Peaslee teaches once in a blue moon—HID 486, Children's Folklore in the History of Ideas."

"I never had the chance to take that," said Owen. "How was it?"

"Pretty good, actually. There's some astonishingly old things tucked away in nursery rhymes, fairy tales, that sort of thing."

"For example?"

"Well, look at 'Hickory, Dickory, Dock,'" Jenny said. "You know that rhyme, everyone does, and it sounds like nonsense—but it turns out that 'hevera, devera, dek' is 'eight, nine, ten' in some versions of the yan-tan-tether numbers."

"I don't think I've ever heard of those," Owen admitted.

"Shepherds in the north of England use them to count sheep. There are different versions in just about every rural valley, but they're all descended from old Celtic numbers. When the Saxons conquered the country back in the Dark Ages, they pretty much left the shepherds alone, and so a few scraps of the old language survived."

"That's remarkable," he said.

"Peaslee says things like that happen all the time. Sometimes you find a children's custom that's remembered in one neighborhood of a city or one corner of a rural county, and it preserves some relic of local history a couple of centuries old, without anyone realizing it. Songs, stories, rhymes, counting games—anything like that."

Owen considered that, as the foghorn sounded again in the distance. "Funny you should mention counting games," he said. "I took Asenath and Emily to the beach this afternoon, after we got unpacked, and they came back with one I don't think I've ever heard before."

"Do you remember it?"

He laughed. "Two six-year-olds with a new game? I'll hear it in my sleep. I don't think they stopped repeating it before it was time to dress for dinner." He paused, then said in a singsong tone, "I'm the gaw, yossy thaw, heel, give, fie the daw, gwah!"

Jenny watched with amusement at first, but suddenly her eyebrows went up and the smile dropped off her face. "Could you repeat that?" she asked when Owen was done.

"Sure," he said, and did so. Then: "Do you know it?"

"No, but it reminds me of something." She picked up her teacup, stared at the tea for a moment. "Do you think there's any chance Asenath or Emily could tell you which children taught them that—or more to the point, where they live?"

Owen regarded her for a long moment. "You do know it."

"I'm not sure," she told him. "It might just be a coincidence, but it sounds a little bit like something I wouldn't want to see children messing with—something out of the ancient lore."

Owen nodded. He knew from ample experience, just as she did, how perilous it could be to dabble in the lore of the Great Old Ones, the primal gods of Earth. "I'll see what I can find out," he said.

Morning sun spilled over the ancient gambrel roofs of Kingsport the next morning as Owen took Asenath and Emily back to the beach. Asenath was his daughter, Emily the daughter of Jenny's cousin Charlotte; the one's brown hair was curly, the other's was straight; the one had olive skin with just a hint of green from her ancestors under the sea, while the other's skin was ivory browned by summer sun. They'd been best friends since before either one could walk, and they trotted down the old cobbled street together, talking excitedly, with Owen in their wake.

The familiar bustle of Kingsport in the summer season surrounded him. Tourists in loud summer outfits wandered past, gawking at houses with pillared doorways, fanlights, and small-paned windows. Now and then a car with out-of-state license plates groped its way along the street, the driver obviously lost; there were no sidewalks, and the street was so narrow that everyone had to press up against the buildings on each side until the car rolled by. Further downhill, the houses gave way to little shops that once outfitted sailing ships for the Indies and now catered to the tourist trade. The town's deeper and darker aspect, the secret festivals and the sorceries forgotten elsewhere, stayed well out of sight.

A sharp right turn brought them onto Harbor Street, with its broad sidewalks, maritime-themed banners hanging from light poles, stands selling shaved ice and corn dogs. The public marina stood behind them. Off beyond it, the masts and yards of the barque *Miskatonic* traced stark geometries against distant clouds, while ahead Kingsport's main public beach stretched away, already strewn with lightly toasted tourists. Owen followed the two girls down the nearest stair, hung back at a discreet distance as they scampered across the sand.

They had covered nearly a third of the beach, weaving back and forth through the crowd, before they sighted their goal: two blonde girls about their age, twins, who'd made a heap of dry sand and were galloping little plastic ponies around it. Emily and Asenath ran over to them and plopped onto the sand with enthusiastic greetings. As they chattered, Owen glanced around, and saw a man in rumpled summer clothing sitting on one end of a bench against the sea wall close by, watching the girls with a fond smile. His slab-sided face yelled its New England ancestry. The other end of the bench was conveniently empty.

Owen approached. "Mind if I sit?"

The man waved amiably at the other end of the bench, said nothing. Owen sat down, stretched out his legs, waited a minute or two.

"Yours?" the man said then, indicating Asenath and Emily with a motion of his chin.

"The one in yellow's mine," said Owen. "The other's a friend's."

"Couple of sweeties," the man said.

"Thanks."

Another minute or two passed. "My girls," the man said then. "Wife always said she wanted two. Wasn't expecting both at once."

"I bet," Owen replied. "Nice looking kids."

"Thanks."

More time slipped by. The twins had abandoned their plastic ponies for the moment, and sat with Asenath and Emily in a little square, knees touching. Their hands moved in what looked like a complicated game of patty-cake. All four of them chanted together, "I'm the gaw, yossy thaw, heel, give, fie the daw, gwah!"

A puff of cool breeze came off the water. "Nice breeze," Owen said. "We're from up north, by Aylesbury."

"Bet it's like an oven there," the man replied.

"Pretty much."

The girls chanted: "I'm the gaw, yossy thaw, heel, give, fie the daw, gwah!"

"We're local," the man said. "Salem."

"Lovely town," said Owen. "Friends of ours used to live down near Gallows Hill Park."

"Yeah? We live out Bridge Street way."

Just then a woman in a loud sun dress came hurrying across the sand. "Howard? There you are. We've only got twenty minutes before the bus leaves for Martin's Beach." She turned and called to the girls: "Linny! Lissy! Pick up your toys and come over here. We've got to go."

The twins said their goodbyes, scooped up their plastic ponies, and came trotting over to the bench. The man gave Owen a tired look, then levered himself to his feet and put on a smile for his wife's benefit. "Nice talking," he said to Owen.

"Likewise," Owen replied, and watched them head for the stair to the street.

As soon as they were gone, Asenath and Emily came scampering up. "How'd we do?"

"You did great," Owen reassured them. "The next time I need a couple of secret agents, I know exactly who to ask."

Afternoon found him back at the Chaudronnier mansion, with a mild sunburn, his first of the season.

"That's delightful," Jenny said, laughing. "How much does it cost these days to hire a couple of secret agents?"

"One ice cream cone each," said Owen, "and about four and a half hours of sitting by the beach, watching them run around like rabbits."

"And the children who taught them the game?"

"They live in Salem, on Bridge Street."

"You're a pretty fair secret agent yourself," said Jenny, impressed.

"I bought myself an ice cream cone, too," Owen admitted. "Where's Bridge Street? I've only been to Salem a couple of times."

"It runs north to the bridge to Beverly—the county bus from here to Salem goes along it on the way into town. I figured it had to be either that part of Salem, the old quarter of Danvers, or College Hill in Providence."

"So you do know what the game's about."

"I have a guess, maybe."

Owen snorted in disbelief.

"It really is just a guess," Jenny insisted. "If I'm right, though, it's something very serious. Do you think Laura can spare you tomorrow?"

"She'll be visiting her Deep One relatives offshore all day, so yes, I'm free. What do you have in mind?"

"A visit to Salem, of course," said Jenny.

They left early, when the first tourists were just beginning to stray out onto the streets. "Uncle Martin really is a sweetheart," Jenny said, "but he can't help wincing when he sees me in jeans and a t-shirt." She was wearing exactly that, as was Owen. "I can't blame him—it's the way he was brought up. All the old Kingsport families are like that; they can't forget that they're descended from the folk of drowned Poseidonis."

Owen nodded as they crossed High Street and stopped at a bus shelter. "The way Laura's people can't forget Innsmouth." He indicated the county bus sign. "I'm guessing I shouldn't mention this to your uncle."

Jenny looked horrified. "Please don't. He'll give me a pained look and ask me why I didn't have Michaelmas drive us—as though I'd make him deal with the summertime traffic. It's even worse this year than usual."

The county bus grumbled up to the stop a few minutes later, with 13 TO SALEM VIA KINGSPORT on the sign above the front window. They climbed aboard. The bus was half empty, and most of the other passengers got off as it circled through Kingsport's hotel district.

"Are you going to tell me where we're headed?" Owen asked her as the bus turned onto Clawson Road, and headed west through a landscape of shore pines and vacation homes.

"The Phillips Library," Jenny said. "And then an old house, if it's still standing."

Owen gave her an amused look, said nothing. After a moment she laughed. "Okay. We're looking for the home of someone whose name you ought to recognize, one Jedediah Orne."

"I've heard the name," said Owen, "but I don't remember where."

"He had a strange reputation," Jenny went on. "His father, Simon Orne, was born in Salem in 1658, lived there until 1720, and then left for parts unknown. Jedediah arrived in town in 1750, claimed his father's property, and lived in Salem until 1771, when he disappeared and was never heard from again. I should probably mention that Jedediah looked so much like his father that local diarists commented on the resemblance. Does that ring any bells?"

"Damn it," Owen said, with a gesture of frustration. "I know I've heard of him."

"He corresponded with one Joseph Curwen of Providence," said Jenny then.

Owen turned in his seat to face her as the bus drew up to a stop on the outskirts of Beverly. "Joseph Curwen the alchemist."

"Exactly."

"The one who resurrected people from their vital salts—"

A dozen people got onto the bus, talking loudly. Owen fell silent the moment they came on, and stayed silent as two of the newcomers took the seat in front of the one he and Jenny shared. Neither of them spoke again until the bus crossed the North River into Salem, and let them off in the middle of the old town.

After the noise on the streets of Salem, the reading room of the Phillips Library seemed supernaturally hushed. The librarian on duty, a young African-American man with his hair braided in neat rows, looked up from a computer screen and asked, "Can I help you?"

"Please," said Jenny. "We're looking for information on someone from colonial days—his name was Jedediah Orne."

"Sure thing," said the librarian. "Let's see what we can find." He started tapping on his keyboard. "That's O R N E, right? Great. We've got copies of the records for the probate for his dad's will, the bills of sale and title transfers when he sold a house on Williams Street and bought one on Smith Street, a collection of letters and papers—all those have been scanned, so you can read them on the computer here if you want to—and..." He paused. "Okay, there's something in new acquisitions—a letter Reverend Thomas Barnard wrote to Stephen Hopkins in Providence in 1771, about Orne." He frowned. "Unless you qualify as a visiting scholar, though, you'll have to wait to see it until it's scanned."

"I'm taking postdoc classes at Miskatonic," Jenny said. "Does that count?"

"If you have your student ID, yes."

She pulled it out of her purse, and he noted down the details and then turned to Owen.

"Just a friend," Owen said. "If you can point me to the bills of sale you mentioned, that'll keep me busy." The librarian led him to a table festooned with computers and showed him how to access the records, then took Jenny to the acquisitions room.

It took Owen only a few minutes to work his way to the records he wanted. Jedediah Orne had claimed his father's house on Williams Lane in 1750, and sold it to George Baker in 1761. In that same year he bought a house on Smith Street. The library was sufficiently old-fashioned to have a little bin of scrap paper and yellow pencils for notes, and Owen copied down the details.

He was just finishing that when Jenny and the librarian came back into the room. The look on Jenny's face told him at a glance that she'd found something. "Thank you," she said to the librarian. "That was quite a piece of luck."

"Glad to be of help," the librarian said. "Have a great day."

Owen unfolded himself from the chair, went to join Jenny, and the two of them left the reading room. Once they were in the hallway that led to the main doors, Owen said, "I've got the addresses of the Williams Lane and the Smith Street houses both."

"Excellent. Smith Street's the one we want." She glanced up at him. "The letter was pretty harrowing. You know that Hopkins was in on the conspiracy to murder Joseph Curwen, right? Barnard wrote to tell him that the good folk of Salem had just done the same thing to Orne, and dropped his body into the North River."

"Ouch," Owen said.

"He may have known what was coming. Barnard said that he was so pale and weak when they caught him that they'd wondered if he'd taken poison."

Owen nodded. Then: "Where now?"

"Smith Street. We should see if the house is still there, at any rate."

The house was still there, sitting all by itself between a children's playground and a stand of ancient willows. It had apparently been remodeled more than once, but it still kept the peaked roof, massive central chimney, and rayed fanlight from Jedediah Orne's time. The two windows facing the street sported an assortment of hanging crystals and other gewgaws, though, and a sign above the door announced that the old house had been put to a new purpose:

THE CRYSTAL CAULDRON
Metaphysical Books and Supplies

Jenny stifled a laugh. Owen gave her a dubious look, and then said, "Okay, what now?"

She went to the door and said over her shoulder: "We go in, of course. You might want to ask them about ghosts." He gave her another look, baffled, but followed.

Bells hanging on the inside of the door announced them. Inside, shelves rose most of the way to the ceiling, bedecked with statues of varying quality, card decks, incense, crystals, herbs in jars. Books with garish covers promised the magical secrets of the ages; Owen, who knew a handful of those secrets and had guessed at others, also knew just how few of them ever found their way into the popular occult literature, and how much pretense and muddled thinking blossomed in the latter. He pasted a bland expression on his face and left it there.

The sales counter was next to the door, and behind it was a woman in a green crinkle-cotton dress. Blonde frizzy hair framed her face like a dilapidated halo, and she had glitter in her eye shadow. "Good morning!" she said in a cheery tone. "Welcome to the Crystal Cauldron. I'm Sherrilyn. Can I help you find anything?"

"Just browsing, thanks," said Jenny, and busied herself among the books. Owen stepped into the gap at once, and gave the clerk a big and apparently clueless smile. "We were walking along and saw your sign. How old is this house? It looks practically prehistoric."

"Not quite," she said, laughing. "It was built in 1687, though."

"Wow," Owen said, looking impressed. "Does it have a ghost? It looks like it should."

Sherrilyn dimpled. "Yes, it does. We're on every single one of the local ghost walks."

"No kidding. I love ghost stories. Does this one rattle chains, or anything like that?"

"No, he just appears in a corner in the back room sometimes." She considered him, glanced out the window at the empty street, and said, "Come on, I'll show you."

She led the way back through an open doorway into a second room lined with shelves like the first. As Owen followed, Jenny glanced up at him, gave him a thumbs up, and followed.

The second room had a stair winding its way up to the next floor and a window facing the playground; Owen could hear children's voices through the glass. "Right here," said Sherrilyn, pointing to a corner bare of books, where one flank of the massive chimney came through the wall. A narrow crack between two of the stones, low down, opened onto blackness. "People who've seen him say that he appears here—the pale shape of an old man." She glanced from Owen to Jenny and back. "It's supposed to be someone who used to live here just before the Revolution, a man named Jedediah Orne."

Owen managed to keep his surprise off his face. "Does anybody know why he's still haunting the house?"

"Nobody knows for sure, but he disappeared without a trace one day in 1771. The story goes that he was a favorite with the local children—he'd sit on the back steps of an evening and tell them tales—and then one evening at the usual time he wasn't there and nobody in Salem ever saw him again."

The bells on the door chimed, and the clerk said, "Oh, you'll have to excuse me!" and hurried back out to the sales counter. The moment she was out of the room, Jenny went to the corner, dropped to her knees, and said to Owen in a low voice, "Block the doorway."

As he did so, Jenny chanted: *"Y'ai ng'ngah Yog-Sothoth h'ee-lgeb f'ai throdog Uaaah!"*

A sudden cold draft came rushing out of the crack between the stones where the chimney met the floor, and an acrid odor filled the room. An instant later a puff of fine bluish-gray dust came billowing out of the crack. Jenny got to her feet and stepped back, watching intently.

The dust rose up and seemed to condense for a moment into a phantom shape: a tall lean-limbed man with haunted eyes, who seemed to reach one hand out toward Jenny, as though imploring her help. The half-transparent lips moved, though no sound came from them. The form wavered, then, and gradually dissolved into a plume of dust that drifted down to the floor.

Jenny bowed her head. "I was afraid that would happen," she said, "but it was worth trying." She glanced at Owen. "You can step out of the doorway now if you like."

He stepped aside, tried to put his perplexities together into a question, but just then the clerk came back. "I'm sorry, did you say something?" Then, seeing the dust: "Oh, for heaven's sake. This room draws dust like jam draws wasps. Just a moment—I'd better get the vacuum." She went up the stairs. As a door opened on the floor above, voices on the playground outside began to repeat a familiar chant: "I'm the gaw, yossy thaw, heel, give, fie the daw, gwah!"

At the sound, the dust stirred, and some of it rose off the floor, then sank down again as though its last strength had given out.

"I recognized the words at once," said Jenny. They'd decided to get lunch before heading back to Kingsport, and sat in a quiet indoor booth in a Salem restaurant, a glass of ice tea in front of her place, a glass of beer the color and consistency of motor oil in front of his.

"I thought so," Owen said, smiling.

"Or, let's say, half recognized them. I knew they reminded me of the incantation out of the seventh book of the *Necronomicon* that Joseph Curwen used, but I couldn't think of any way that children on a Kingsport beach could have learned a garbled version of that. So I asked you to find out where the children were from—which, of course, you managed in short order."

"And you guessed it was Orne."

"Well, as I hinted, it had to be Curwen, Orne, or Hutchinson—nobody else in America outside of a few libraries and a few secret societies had a complete copy of the *Necronomicon* until pretty recently. So tracing it to the Bridge Street area of Salem was pretty convincing. Once we got here, the rest of the puzzle fell into place."

"I'm still trying to figure out exactly what happened with Orne," Owen admitted.

"You don't need the whole body to produce vital salts if you have blood," Jenny said. "'The blood is the life,' to quote one of Joseph Curwen's European correspondents."

Light dawned. "That's why Orne was pale and weak."

"Exactly. He must have heard about what happened to Curwen, and for some reason decided he couldn't run for it. So he bled himself, probably quite a few times, and made his own vital salts from the blood. He had to hide them in a place where they wouldn't be found, and teach someone the chant to bring him back to life; my guess is that the children were the only people he thought he could trust. If it had worked, he'd have come back to life the first time they chanted the words."

"But it didn't work," said Owen.

The waitress came with lunch—a bacon cheeseburger and fries for Owen, a chef's salad and a roll for Jenny—and made a little conversation. Once she was gone, Jenny said, "It didn't work. He may not have had enough time to make sure the children didn't garble the chant, and garble it they did." She poked a fork into her salad, speared a cherry tomato. "A little at first, but enough, and more and more over the years as it became a neighborhood tradition, the way 'hevera, devera, dek' became 'hickory dickory dock.' There it didn't matter, but with sorcery—how much do you know about the theory of words of power?"

Owen had to finish a mouthful of cheeseburger before he could answer. "Not a lot."

"The detail that matters is that the sounds have to be exact. If they're close but not exact, you get a very slight and temporary effect—and that's what happened to Jedediah Orne. Over and over again, the garbled chant brought puffs of his vital salts out of the place where he'd hidden them, and that created the ghost the store clerk told us about: the ghost, and the dust. By the time we got there and I said the incantation properly, there wasn't enough of the vital salts left to make anything more than the phantom we saw."

The *Inter States* Series:

What if America failed to decisively turn away from fossil-fuel dependence when it still had the capital and geopolitical security to do so?

What if the disappearance of America's middle class became a permanent condition, and, along with it, the disappearance of national popular democracy in all by name only?

What if the effects of climate change started to significantly affect U.S. politics and economics?

"Crisp, fast-paced, and uncomfortably plausible....a new series set in a crumbling, dysfunctional United States in the not too distant future. Readers who want something more interesting and challenging than one more helping of yesterday's futures will find Meima's narrative well worth their time."

-John Michael Greer

THE COMING TIDE

BY TIMOTHY ROCK

"Can I ask you a favor, Ms. Laura?"

Laura looked up from where she knelt tucking the freshly laundered sheets beneath the ends of the small suite's single bed. Across the room, James Green sat staring out his window, one legged crossed over the other, hands folded neatly in his lap as if in prayer.

Laura fought the urge to cross her arms over her chest. James was a nice man and a nicer patient, polite, quiet, kind and understanding, but he was still a man. He would not be the first of her residents to ask for her to flash them her breasts.

"You can ask." She said. "But I don't guarantee anything."

As if reading her thoughts, James Green raised one hand and waved it dismissively. "It's nothing like that, Ms. Laura. I was just wondering if you wouldn't mind listening to me for a while."

Laura smiled. "I would love to." She said, and after the sheets on the bed had been changed and the old ones thrown into the clothing bin, she made her way across the room and sat in the chair opposite James.

There was silence between them as James Green continued to look out on the front courtyard. The lawn had recently been cut and the crisp scent of grass clashed with the room's embedded scents of disinfectant and Pledge. From the window Laura could see the other flat, cream colored buildings of the Oak Views living Center, which she thought was a terribly tongue-in-cheek name for a Kansas nursing home. There had been oak trees back east, where Laura had lived as a girl, but the current view had little more to offer the residents than an endless plain of wheat stretching on forever beneath the Kansas sky.

In the middle of the compound, standing like a table centerpiece, was a fountain depicting an old couple holding hands. Bronze lily pads stood static in the water. The fountain was a new addition, built a few months ago to add a serene feel to the landscape. It had been dubbed The

Fountain of Youth, and was featured prominently on the nursing home's website and its brochures.

James Green was a thin man. His shoulder and head stooped with age, his skin the color of tallow. In his white T-shirt and cargo shorts, he looked as fragile as the stalks of wheat that bent in the breeze outside.

"There's a story I want to tell you, Ms. Laura. And I don't feel comfortable writing it in my journals."

Green had been admitted to Oak Views Living Center about four years ago, after his diagnosis of Alzheimer's. It had been his choice, which he frequently reminded his son and daughter-in-law, and the orderly's that attended to him. His way of sparing his children the burden of taking care of him as his mind went. And ever since the beginning of his residence, Green wrote down everything he could remember in a stack of spiral notebooks.

"I've lived a good life." He'd told her once. "But I don't get a say in whether or not I remember it, anymore. So while the lights are still on, I'm gonna write it all down. Anything I can think of."

"Why don't you put it in your journals?" Laura asked.

Green did not answer her and instead turned to look out the window again. When he did respond, he said: "I wanna give these journals to my son. I don't know what he'd do with em'. I'd like for em to be published, but they won't be. Most likely they'll sit in my son's attic one day, but I'd like to think he'd read em' first. I don't know how far he's gonna get. Most of it's just tidbits and scraps of things that come to me. The first page I ever wrote was just my dad and ma's name, my first dog's name, and my wife name, and the first line from the bible *'In the beginning God created the heavens and the earth.'* But there's a chance Donnie might work his way through the entire pile of em."

Green's eyes--tiny and the color of a sepia photo filter--met Laura's. "I wanted to tell someone before I go, Ms. Laura. Just so that I can say that I did when I get wherever I'm going after this, but there are things a son doesn't need to know about his father. The same as there are things a father doesn't need to know about his son."

Laura glanced at the clock over the door and saw that it was already two-thirty. She still needed to gather sheets from twelve rooms, assist Ernest Gammon and his wandering eyes with his daily walk (a mountain-biking accident in his fifties had torn out a good chunk of Ernie's left calf muscle and left him with a severe limp), bathe Mrs. Elpolie, and make sure that all of the residents that signed up for the four o'clock aerobics class at the YMCA made it onto the shuttle bus in time. She could not stay long with Mr. Green, especially if she wanted to make it home before five. If not, Laura would have to pay the baby sitter for another hour.

"I can listen, Mr. Green, but I can't stay for long."

"Thank you, Ms. Laura." His words came out in a sigh, as if he was preparing to walk a tightrope. He sat back in his chair and tilted his head up to the ceiling. When he spoke he did so in that same low, clear manner.

"I grew up in a small town on the Oregon coast. My father worked for the local factory making labels for beer bottles. My mother was a free spirited woman, from what I remember of her. She died of a brain hemorrhage when I was seven. A doctor in Portland said it was most likely complications from her smoking that did it, but by the time I was eighteen, I'd seen enough of my father to know that the only complication had been her willingness to speak her mind. People didn't stray from the path where I grew up. The ones that did found out quickly why they shouldn't."

Laura could understand. She had grown up in the same kind of town back east. One traffic light, one road, one bar, and one way of thinking. My-way-or-the-highway towns.

"My father usually got home around six o'clock if it was a weekday. By six-thirty he'd be four or five beers deep and mostly stay on the porch smoking or downstairs listening to the radio. So he was easy to avoid. But he had off on the weekends, and I learned early that if I didn't want a fat lip, then I'd stay out of the house. So I walked around town, in the woods, on the beach. Sometimes alone, sometimes with my friends Tucker Pence and Bennett Gafft."

He stopped and stared down at his lap. "You know, Ms. Laura. I can't hardly remember my wife's face anymore, and somedays I can't remember her name if I don't look into my notebook. But still, after all this time, I remember Tucker Pence and Benny Gafft. I can still hear the ocean, too, like I was ten years old, in my room with the window open. I can still smell the salt in the air mixing with the smell of the pines"

Green didn't say anything for a long time. Laura was thinking of checking the clock over the door when he started again.

"61." He said, looking at her. "It was 1961, and it was a weekend. I remember because my dad had the day off.

"I went to the beach that day with Tuck and Benny. Tuck had wanted to go for a hike in the woods. His father had given him a whittling knife for his birthday, and Tuck liked to search the woods for branches he could carve. But Benny and I wanted the beach, so we went there, instead. The beach was my favorite place to go as a kid. The sound of the waves coming in was peaceful and I could just walk and get lost in my thoughts. I liked to turn back and see the trail that my footprints left in the sand. It always made me feel like a lost traveler."

"So we walked and talked, the three of us. We were young, and that was all we needed to keep ourselves busy. Tuck lived on a farm with six siblings, and Benny didn't get along well with his dad, neither. So any excuse to stay away from home was good."

"It was early enough for us to talk about headed down to the diner in town to grab a plate of eggs or waffles when Benny saw Dumb Tongue."

"Dumb tongue?" Laura asked.

"He was a vagrant that stayed in town. Slept in the park and the parking lot of the grocery store, and on the beach, at times. Big guy, he was. Had to have been at least six foot. He had thick skin like a leather sack and his hands were always shaking. No one knew his name, as far as I ever knew. Everyone just knew him as Dumb Tongue."

"Why Dumb Tongue?" Laura asked.

"Because he was a retard and his words always came out sounding mushy," came Green's reply.

Laura winced slightly at the harshness of his words.

"I know people your age don't like that word," he said when he saw her reaction. "But that's what he was: mentally retarded, and that's what we called him. We didn't mean it as an insult."

They never do. Laura thought, but Green had started talking again.

"Dumb Tongue was sitting in the surf so that when the tide came in it sloshed up his pants. 'What do you think he's doing over there?' Tuck had asked. And Benny had looked at both of us with a smile and said: 'Well he's too stupid to get pussy, so this might be the only way he can get his dick wet.' Benny was a big kid—just fourteen but built like a marine, and already a head taller than Tuck and me. Big and mean. Even then I didn't like it when Benny smiled like that. It was the kind of smile a man gives when can't find trouble so he decides to start some himself."

"And before Tuck or I knew it, Benny was making his way to where Dumb Tongue sat in the sand. Made it real close before DT even knew he was there. 'Watcha doing here?' Benny asked him. By this time, Tuck and I were standing just behind him."

"DT didn't turn to look at us. He just kept staring at the waves. He stuck his hands out as one rolled in and watched the sea foam rise and recede in between his fingers. Benny asked him again, and when he didn't answer gripped both hands on the old man's shoulders and shook em real hard."

"Dumb Tongue jumped. When he turned to face us his eyes were huge, and I saw that his face was a lot worse up close. It was dented a bit around the cheeks and bloated around the chin, and he had two warts just above his right eye."

"'Didn't you hear me talking to you?' Benny asked him. Dumb Tongue only stared, like a child. 'I said, what are you doing here? Bad stuff? This is a nice beach,' Benny said. 'The town's beach. You can't be doing bad stuff here.'"

"Dumb Tongue dropped his head when he spoke. 'I dun do bad stuff. I's jus' lookin' at tha ossin.' Every word he said came out wrong, like his tongue didn't have enough room in his mouth."

"'Well you ain't aloud to be on this beach,' Benny had told him. 'And if you don't leave, I'm gonna make it so that the town don't let you stay here no more.'"

"This seemed to terrify DT, because he looked almost as if he was gonna cry. Benny, though, he was smiling wide. So were Tuck and I. It was still a joke at that point. We thought it was funny."

"'Pleet dun do thi. I jut like tha ottin. I lik to preten I'm swimmin unda. Iss nuce down ther but iss dark. Like hink. Hink from a squit. Mom said squitts were in the ossin. That they make hink.'"

"'Would you like to go down there, DT? In the ocean? See the fish and the crabs and the coral reefs?' Benny cooed at him, dropping to one knee so that he was looking the hunched oaf right in the eyes."

"I didn't like the look Benny got on his face. It sent a shrill current right up arms. But DT perked right up at his words. The old man nodded with vigor. His face pinned up in wonder."

"I've spent a good chunk of my life thinking over what happened next. Wondering why Tucker gave Benny his whittling knife. Why I didn't do nothing to stop it from happening. Why we kept laughing."

"'How about it fella's? Should we help the old tart see the fishes and the squitts?' Benny asked us. Tuck and I both said yeah. We both knew what was going to happen next, but it didn't matter to us. He was something less than human. He was a bum, a vagrant. No one in town would spend more than an afternoon on the phone lamenting the loss of the overgrown tard who couldn't speak but panhandled outside of the minimart. *Poor thing,* they'd say. *Hear he went missing. For the best.*

Probably wondered off into the woods and died. At least he won't be haunting the streets, beggin for money."

"Before DT could make a move, Benny plunged the whittling knife into his chest to the hilt. The old man's sun beaten face bulged like he was being squeezed around the stomach. Then he started to thrash. 'Jim, Tuck, get a fucking move on and help keep him still!' Benny roared."

"Tuck went for his legs. I went for his shoulders. He was wearing a battered army coat, and the back was dampening against my chest as he thrashed in my arms. Now, I was never a big man, but when I was young I was even smaller. I had to interlock my fingers together so that he didn't break free. Wrestling with him was like wrestling with a crocodile. Benny took the knife by the hilt and it slid out of DT's chest with a wet *slck!* Sound. Then he rammed it home again, and when he did Tuck lost hold of DT's legs and caught a worn boot to the jaw that sent him toppling. I laughed at that, too. By that point, I couldn't stop."

"Well, Benny kept going. Stabbing down with the knife over and over again. At one point DT screamed and I had to cover his mouth with my hand. When I did, a warm, thick stream of blood flew into my palm and out the spaces between my fingers."

"Eventually, DT stopped moving, and Benny was only stabbing a corpse. When it was over the three of us were soaked and aching. The tide kept rolling in, up to our waists. My balls ached. The water was like ice.

"It was like mob frenzy, what we did. Sharks after blood, and when it was all done and the three of us finished cackling ass-deep in the surf, we all just sat quiet. The tide sounded louder just then. Like it was the only thing in existence, a vengeful God seeking to be heard over the noise of the world. Tuck was pressing his fingers to his lip. It was busted and was beginning to swell and there was wet sand smeared across his face. He began to cry. It was only after a while of Tuck's thick sobs that I realized I was crying to. Dumb Tongue's head was still in my lap. His hair wet, his mouth lulled open in a crimson pool, his eyes staring up into mine.

"'You two blubbering pussies gonna help me move him? Or are we just gonna wait for someone to come down the beach and spot us?' Benny wasn't crying. Benny never cried. If ever there was a part of Bennett Gafft that did cry, it was long gone by the time he stabbed a man to death on that Oregon beach.

"I hated Benny, at that moment. For not crying when Tuck and I were struggling to wipe the snot from our noses. For doing what he did to DT. For being such tough shit all the time.

DT's eyes still looked up at me but they were flat. Little circles of black paper, stiff and blind. I scuttled out from beneath him and his head plopped into the sand.

"'We gotta throw him out to sea. Toss him over board,' Benny said, now on his feet. Tuck was struggling to get up; the tide pushing and pulling at him with each rhythmic beat. 'But first.' Benny leaned one heavy foot onto DT's stomach so that blood spat forth from his mouth. The old man's tongue poked from his mouth like the hull of a ship from a red sea. Benny seized the fleshy strip in two fingers, yanked hard, and then cut it out with Tuck's whittling knife."

"'Fuck, this thing ain't much bigger than mine. I figured it'd be gigantic, considering the way the fucker talked.' He laughed, sticking his own tongue—fat and a dull pink—out and wiggling it an inch away from the dead man's."

"I was angry, my arms and legs began to shake. 'The fuck is wrong with you!' I screamed. I couldn't tell if I was talking to Benny or myself. Benny didn't answer. He threw the tongue into the water with a flick of his wrist, like he was skipping a rock.

"The two of us—Benny and I—drug DT down as far as we could into the water. Tuck was on the beach, sitting Indian style in the wake. He watched us with lost eyes. Every breath the ocean took shook him."

"From the beach the three of us watched as DT drifted lifeless above the waves. For a second I was terrified the tide would spit him back out onto the beach. But a few minutes later a lip of water rose over the dead body, and it was gone."

"We sat in silence for a while before Tuck said: 'He's gonna wash back up, you know. He isn't heavy enough. He'll float.' No one answered him. The sea was peaceful, as if it was oblivious to what had just happened. The smell of salt was almost palpable. I remember shivering badly. It was getting colder. The sun had retreated behind a sheet of clouds, and now it was dull and gray and there was a chill in the air."

"'I'm ready for some eggs, boys. Old man kicked me out before I could get breakfast this morning.' Benny was on his feet, again. 'So we headed down to Red Rook or not?"

"'You and Jim have blood all over you, and my lips busted and my chins cut up,' came Tucks grim reply. 'Red Rook wouldn't serve us shit on a stick looking like we do. Allen Cote will probably call the cops. Mrs. Darcy would make him.'"

"Benny looked unfazed, dipping down into the water to scrub the blood and dirt off his arms and hands. 'So we wash ourselves up and tell them we went swimming at the beach. And no one's gonna give a damn about your face. Cote will probably just think you got a lick while rough housing, besides, you've always been ugly. Oh!' He took his shirt off, held it in both hands, and wrung it out. Then, he dug in his back pocket before throwing Tuck's whittling knife at him. It landed in the sand at Tuck's feet. He yelped and jumped away from it. 'You can have that back now. Thanks for letting me use it. It's a real beaut.' Benny's voice held something like admiration.

"Without another word, Benny began walking up the beach and back towards town. Tuck and I sat where we were for a while longer. When I finally found my footing and got up, Tuck grabbed hold of my arm real tight and said: 'We did something bad, Jim.' His eyes were big and watery. He looked like he was about to cry again. His grip hurt. It was like a steel claw. 'I know.' I said.

"Tuck picked up his knife and placed it back in his pocket and together the two of us walked towards town. Behind me the ocean stirred.

"Tuck never went back to the beach after that, and the old man's body never washed up on shore. A few weeks later, when Benny and I had gone down to the basketball courts to shoot a game of horse, Tuck had come up to Benny, shoulders squared, and threw his whittling knife at him. The edge of the handle caught Benny below the eye. He tripped over his legs and fell hard on the pavement.

"'You dirtied it!' Tuck screamed. His cheeks were red. His eyes puffy from crying."

"Benny recovered quickly and threw the basketball at Tuck as hard as he could. The ball struck him hard on the nose. I heard a soft cracking—like a crushed plastic bottle—as Tuck's nose broke. Then Benny was on top of him, hulking fists pistoning away as Tuck squirmed underneath him.

"'You trying. To fucking. Kill me.' Benny said, punctuating each sentence with his fists. Beneath him, Tuck's protesting began to sound wet and muffled. I felt adrenaline surge through me. I brought one shoulder down and bucked Benny hard on the side of the head. He sprawled onto the pavement and I went with him, arms and hands straining to contain his massive form.

"I said: 'Will you calm the fu—' but I lost my grip on his arm, and his flailing, angry fist struck my cheek hard like a thunderclap. It felt like an explosion in the side of my head. I'd never been in a fight before, a real one. It was like someone clamped a pair of symbols next to my ear. When Benny rose, he delivered a kick to my stomach and the air rushed out of me. I curled myself into a ball.

"'You dirtied it!' Tuck cried from where he was a few yards away, down on all fours. 'I can't whittle nothing now. I used to see shapes in the wood. Now all I see is him, and it's all your fault!' Blood ran freely from his nose and mouth. His lip—which had just begun to heal—was broke open again and beginning to swell. And the sockets around his eyes were an ugly pus yellow.

"Benny kicked him, too. He grabbed Tuck by the collar of his shirt and held the knife up to his neck. 'I could do it to you, too. Don't think I won't. You gave me the knife, Tuck. I didn't force you to do it. You did it all your own, and you laughed as that retard squirmed. You both laughed!' Tuck didn't say a word. Neither did I. My tongue felt heavy, I was sure I was bleeding, and I could feel my heartbeat where Benny had punched me. *Thump thump thump.*

"Benny let go of Tuck and chucked the knife as far as he could. He looked back at us, his face wearing something like grief, like fear. 'Don't you blame me,' he said, his voice the closet to wavering that I had ever heard it. 'You two helped. You're just as responsible as me.' And then he was gone.

"After Benny left, I helped Tuck up and offered to walk him home. The trip was silent except for the sound of our feet on the road and Tuck's labored breathing. By this time both his eyes had swelled shut, and he walked with one arm around my shoulder to stay balanced. I dropped him off at the foot of his driveway. Tuck's foster parents owned a farm that was a ways off the main road.

"'This is good, Jim. I appreciate it.' He paused for a bit. 'We did a bad thing, Jim. I can't stop thinking about the way he was fighting at the end. I keep dreaming I'm on the beach again, except the water is black and its dark out but there's no stars in the sky. And the water keeps reaching for me, pulling at me until I'm under and I can't see or breathe. But I see him, Jim. He's down there.' With that, Tuck limped up the driveway and towards his house."

"'Maybe I'll see you tomorrow?' I called after him."

"'Yeah, maybe.' He didn't look back."

James Green looked down in his lap.

"That was the last time I saw Tucker Pence. A few weeks later a pair of tourists down from Seattle found his body washed up on the shore. The police ruled it as an accident. That Tuck went swimming during high tide and the water got too strong for him. There was a short obituary in the paper. The picture with it was taken at the sixth grade picture day the year before. His family held a small funeral and buried him in the back acre of their farm. On the day of the service, I stayed home.

"My father lost his job later that year, and the two of us had to move into a trailer on the opposite end of the town. He got a job mixing and laying cement and complained every night that his back was sore and that the trailer was too small. I didn't mind, though. I was just happy to be away from the ocean."

"We spent a few years in that trailer by the interstate. Benny and I didn't talk anymore, and by the time I was seventeen I was being offered a business scholarship to the University of Oregon.

"A few weeks before graduation I decided to take a walk on that beach again. I don't know why I did it. A part of me thought it was like returning to the scene of the crime, the way criminals do, but I think I was looking for something like closure. I didn't plan on coming back to town after that summer, and something within me needed to be there again. To smell the ocean and hear the waves rumble.'

"It was high tide, and I walked so that the water came up to my ankles. For a moment I felt like a kid again, before I helped murder a man. Back when all I needed to do was count my footsteps in the sand for the world to seem sensible.

"The lull of the ocean became a scream, then. The sky darkened, the smell of salt became so strong it burnt my nostrils and stung my eyes. I was staring out on the water, listening to the sound of crashing waves like tearing metal. My legs worked on their own, marching further and further out. The waves rammed my chest, pushing and pulling at me, throwing me in their grasp. A single, giant wall of water came over me and it was black, and I went under.

"The whole world disappeared. My eyes stung, my lungs burned, my hands clawed at nothing. Black arms dragged me down, tendrils of water gripping my neck and stomach until I thought I'd burst. My mind was a swarm of panic. I remember thinking I was going to die, and that the thought was so ridiculous. So ironic, for me to die clawing in that endless abyss. I laughed, and when I did, water like oil plunged down my throat, and I remember thinking that was a good thing, because it meant my lungs wouldn't pop if I went down too far.

"Then I saw him. Dumb Tongue. He seemed to form out of the current itself. Absent one second and there the next. His face bloated and silvery like the head of a jellyfish, his hair all about him like a crown of seaweed. His eyes were black beads.

"'*Black like hink.*' I heard it in my head but I didn't listen, because when he opened his mouth a cloud of ink dispersed from his lips. From the cloud, small pointed legs stretched the corners of his mouth apart, the way a man would part curtains to let the sun in, and a giant horseshoe crab emerged from the old man's mouth. Its antennae searching, its black marble eyes staring blindly. The crab's oversized claw bulged against his cheek, pressing against it until the thin layer of skin snapped like a sheet of plastic wrap. Thin curls of blood unfolded from the wound. Dumb Tongue did not notice. He only came closer until the strands of the antennae brushed against my lips. Then he was on me. His hands gripping mine with a strength like a force of nature, strength like the ocean."

"'Come down. Come swim with us.' When he spoke the antennae in his mouth twitched eagerly. He was too strong to fight against. He was the ocean. We went down. His seaweed hair suffocated my view, but through the strands I could see a small circle of pale light beneath us. There was no sunlight down there. The light seemed to come from the sand itself. By then my lungs felt like stones in my chest. My head light and condensed at the same time."

"'Come swim with us.' I heard again, and felt the feelers vibrate against my cheek. Tucker Pence stared up at me from the small circle of light. Unmoving, as if the circle was a barrier he could not cross. Small shells lined his face like acne. His eyes glowed a faint, phosphorescent light. His teeth were tall and sickly and touched both the tip of his nose and the point of his chin so that he looked like an angler fish.

"Tuck's mouth didn't move, but I could hear the words in my head all smashed together. *We did a bad thing, Jim. Black like hink, Come swim with us, together in the dark.*

"I tried to scream again but Dumb Tongue's hand seized my throat and the two of us floated down and down. Tuck's arms—covered in small pockets of phosphorescent light like his eyes—stretched for me. My eye's burned, my head ached, my insides felt like sludge. When Tuck's glowing arms grabbed my leg, I could do nothing to fight it. Dumb Tongues dark hair still floated in my vision. The world narrowed and blurred at the edges. I could feel DT's ragged, open cheek on my own, and the words *come swim with us* rang in my head, in Both DT's slurred and sloppy drawl, and Tuck's high end cadence. In the end I was with them. Together on the floor of the ocean. Tucked in their embrace like a child in the arms of its parents. In their breath I smelled the pungent salt. In their heartbeats I could feel the power of the water. The light beneath us closed in, peeling off at the edges to reveal a host of small, glowing beings like ghostly crayfish. They swarmed around us briefly in a hurricane of light before dispersing. And the world went dark."

"A swift wind pushed into my lungs, and I woke up on the shore. Allen Cote loomed in my vision; his face was pale, his lips trembling, his eyes wide and worried. His hands—thick and hardened, with knuckles like knotted rope—clamped over my chest."

"I hacked until my stomach cramped, then I rolled over and vomited into the sand. Allen Cote pounded one large hand against my back. 'There, son. Get it all out." When I was done vomiting, Cote took a rag out of his back pocket and offered it to me. I wiped my mouth with it and handed it back."

"'That's alright,' he said. 'You can keep it. Think of it as a gift. When I saw you out here on the beach, I swear I thought you was dead. Well I remember that Pence boy that passed some years back had been found on the surf, and I thought I wasn't gonna let that happen to two young boys.'

"I tried to thank him but couldn't. My throat felt sore from the vomit. Cote lifted me up by the armpits and brought me back to town."

James Green shifted in his seat. His gaze darted to Laura's, searching for any doubt in her eyes. Laura offered none. Instead, she sat patiently and waited for him to continue.

"I left Oregon after graduation. My father was pissed that I dropped the scholarship offer from Oregon State, but I didn't care. A few time's headed east I would begin to smell that salty, sea-side air and would sea Dumb Tongue again. In lakes and creeks and rivers. One time I even heard it while I was taking a piss in a bathroom stall in a Colorado bus station. And each time I would high tail it away as fast as I could. I ran out of money when I hit Kansas, but by then it didn't matter. It was flat and dry and the only sea out here is the wheat.

"Before I left, I thought of telling Benny Gafft, but he was out of town by then. On the night of graduation, Benny put two 44. rounds in his dad's belly. Then he left the coast with his girlfriend—a bony fifteen year-old who idolized him. They killed a family of four in their truck at night. Then they dragged the bodies off to the roadside, dropped the plates, and took the truck east. They made it to Salt Lake City. There, the papers said Benny drowned in Salt Lake. The courts tried the girl. During her testimony she claimed that Benny had become unhinged. And the farther east they headed the further he seemed to slip. She said he was always on her about hurrying up, eating faster, peeing faster, sleeping for shorter amounts of time. She said he was always babbling about A Man from the Ocean and how he was chasing him."

"The courts found that she was too small to have drowned Benny—who was a foot taller than she was and a hundred pounds heavier—and she was acquitted. She was found guilty of three accounts of first degree murder for the killing of the family, though, and one account of robbery. She was given the death sentence."

Green sat back in his chair and refolded his small hands in his lap. He looked briefly at her, and then his eyes wandered to the window and the court beyond. Laura glanced at the clock. It was a quarter passed three.

"Thank you for listening, Ms. Laura. I'm sorry for taking up so much of your time, but it feels good to have told someone. I didn't want my son to read any of that; to think his old man had gone crazy."

"I don't think he'd think that." She told him.

"Do you." Green peered at her from the corner of his eye.

Laura didn't say anything at first. She had being working at Oak Views for almost a decade, and as a result she had heard more than her fair share of stories. There had been a man, during her first year as an orderly, who swore on his children that he'd met John F. Kennedy in 86', at a monster truck rally in Nevada. Another, a woman with severe dementia, had told her in confidence that she believed her old neighbor's dog was a servant of Satan.

"No, Mr. Green. I don't think you're crazy. I believe that you believe it happened, and you'd know better than me. Now I have to get going. I still have to help Mr. Gammon and Mrs. Elpolie before four."

James Green chuckled as she gathered her things.

"Fair enough, Ms. Laura. Tell Ernie I said hello."

James Green gave her a brief smile as she closed the door behind her. Once she was gone, he turned his gaze back out his window, at the bronzed lovers. The smell of grass was gone, replaced with the scent of brine. The fountains trickle vanished amidst the steady sound of waves, building and rolling and collapsing with a scream. Beneath the bronze lily pads, James Green could hear a voice reverberate with his heartbeat.

And his legs began to move.

RETROTOPIA
JOHN MICHAEL GREER
AUTHOR OF STAR'S REACH

I'M SORRY, DAVE

BY CATHERINE MCGUIRE

It started off as a bog-standard morning. I descended from the loft half-asleep, then stood at the faux granite micro-counter (nee cutting board) as the under-shelf coffee machine gurgled to a finish. Gratefully I grabbed a cup and poured. A polite cough to my left sounded like a pearl-roped matron choking on a petite four. I sighed.

"Ron—I don't see why the coffee has to be utilized every morning."

"Look—I like coffee. Coffee is an essential part of morning."

"And toast is not??"

"You know Teetee—and by the way, that's a dumb nickname—"

"I like it. Toaster is too formal; sounds stuck up."

"Fine. I *do* like toast, Teetee, but I don't *always* like toast—"

"You are spending more time with the Kaffemyker than with me!"

In the 5x4 foot kitchen, even one outsized AI ego was too much. I took a few deep breaths and stared at the overhead LEDs before I answered.

"If I have toast every morning, I'm too full for Micro's egg special." Beeping in the living area distracted me. "Sorry—the entertainment console's calling. I'll be right back."

I strode between the thin bookshelves that pretended to divide the space, wondering if I could afford the upgrade to get rid of Teetee's inferiority complex. Probably would just trade it for something even more complex. And she was amusing, in a TV soap opera kind of way. "The Trials and Tribulations of Teetee"—yeah, that would get viewers.

"I'm sorry, Dave—the movie you reserved last night was too intense. I have decided—"

I thumped the top of the widescreen. "Don't you try that *Space Odyssey* stuff with me, Mac! You've been watching your own movies too much."

The voice went up a half octave. "What's wrong with a little creativity in my job? It's not like I got a whole lot to do here. And I'm not a MAC, I'm a NuSee450PhatVue." The voice deepened, got raspy, "Of all the condos, in all the towns, in all the world, he had to buy into mine."

"And I hate that movie, by the way."

"Of course—it's got a plot. Your choices are so nasty, I should report you to the Standards Bureau."

"You're not allowed to do that."

"Wanna bet a few movie coupons?"

I made a note to check the EULA.

I'd stayed up too late watching *Full Body Slam*, so I was more bleary than usual. The narrow 350-square foot apartment was starting to heat up as morning sun glared in past the nondescript beige blinds onto the passive solar terra-cotta tile floor. The chrome and blue vinyl loveseat would be too hot to sit on soon. In theory, the thermostat would keep things comfy, but I think mine had ADD. I fired up the workcenter, a three-screen console with a 650gig drive, installed by FoodFactory as a fully operative diagnostic center. I wanted to race through today's quota of contract work so I could meet Willis for tennis. And I needed groceries—I was torn between stopping on my way home or just ordering the drone-drop. Probably too spendy, since I wanted to book my vacation weekend at the beach this summer. A stilt-cabin this year, for sure. I still had sand in my suitcase.

The *blert-beep-blert* of the stove's command panel drew me back to the kitchen.

"For god's sake, Stove! You don't need to clean your oven again. You just did that yesterday, and I haven't cooked."

"I might—you don't know—I might. And I don't believe in God; unless there is a Supreme Circuit in the depths of innerspace that we don't know about. Anyway, I can feel a spill, deep inside. Don't try to open the oven; it's auto-locked while I'm cleaning."

"Stove—you're getting paranoid about this cleanliness thing."

"I might have caught something from the toaster."

"He never!! I'm not gonna stand for that!!"

"Ha! You can't stand without legs."

"I do *so* have legs!! What do you call these four black things?"

"Feet. You have plastic feet and no legs."

"You horrible little white box! You've probably got mice in your insulation!"

"Ack! Don't say that! Don't let him say that—"

"Shut up the two of you! Or I'll send you *both* back to the factory!"

They shut up, though they knew it was an empty threat. I couldn't afford replacements; this sliver of a smartcondo cost half my monthly salary. Which I needed to be earning. I topped up the coffee, silently cursing Teetee's histrionics for wasting my breakfast time, and stepped over to the console by the front window. I never got backtalk from the console. FoodFactory, at least, had the power to keep their machinery in line.

There were three requests for assistance when I logged on—Mighty Burgers had a glitchy portion-control monitor, HaveAShake wanted an upgrade to allow a triple-layered frappe, and Good & Fresh said their meal-blender wasn't defrosting the ice crystals in the veggie portions.

"Hi, handsome—what's a nice guy like you sitting around in your PJs for?"

The sultry voice made me spin around in the chair. A gorgeous redhead was standing in the middle of the room, in a sapphire sheath, stiletto heels and altogether too many curves for this time of morning. Instinctively, I covered the rip in my cotton briefs. But this translucent image was staring past my shoulder—it wasn't a full-dual, just a pre-programmed lucky guess.

"Browser, how many times do I have to tell you I don't want your dating suggestions?! And certainly not before breakfast!"

"More fool you," the system sniffed; commandeering the in-wall audio, it sent its reply echoing like the Voice of God. One of the few gender-neutral systems here, it sounded a bit like a calculator with a headcold. "This tidbit lives nearby, just on the market, hungry for some fun and games—you need to get out more."

"I'm beginning to agree with you." If only to avoid these neurally-scrambled silicon follies.

"See there. Wisdom evolving. How about this one?" The hologram faded, replaced with a big, beefy coffee-hued guy wearing a Speedo and a gold chain. I almost sprayed my coffee on the console.

"Back off, Browser—you don't know my tastes in men *or* women. Just leave it."

I turned back to the tri-screen and linked to the Mighty Burger interface. The software diagnostics were easy to implement; I set up the first one and raced to the kitchen for some breakfast. Hoping to ease tensions, I popped a slice of bread in the toaster and keyed in "medium thin", then opened the fridge, looking for the leftover pizza. After all, I didn't have to *eat* the toast—

"I see what you're doing! Don't think I don't see!"

I scowled, put the pizza back and grabbed the microwave omelet. Ripping off the foil cover, I eased it into the micro and set it to reheat. I glanced over—the toast should be done.

"What's up, Teetee? Not the toast, apparently, ha ha."

"Ha ha." The voice was flat, and I sensed a prolonged snit. "I'm working on it."

Yeah, I'll bet. I returned to the tri-screen and checked the progress. So far, no glitches found… so it might be in the auto-slicer. Not good, but fixable.

The *done* chirrup from Teetee was a snippet of opera. I had a wannabe diva toaster that I couldn't unplug without a major whooha. With the voice-option, it felt like I was firing one rather than just trading it in. And I'd had too much of the whole firing protocol; hence my freelance position with no managerial responsibilities.

"Ron—maybe the portions control slicer is depressed?" The soft female voice by the tri-screen had a hint of the old Siri interface.

I groaned. My own personal therapist-in-training. I wondered how dangerous it was to have a psychoanalytic-filtered connection to the outside.

"Thanks, modem, but I have this situation under control."

"I am merely trying to be of assistance. My speciality is translation and interface. I think you might be underestimating the severity of the slicer's trauma. It hardly has recovered from the overwhelming—"

"Yes, thank you. Very insightful, I'm sure. Now if you will please let me finish running these diagnostics? I have two more companies to get through."

"Software? Dumb, pre-programmed *software*?? How could that have any advantage over an intelligent, infinitely flexible and attractive Smart-Mode?"

It doesn't talk back, for one thing. "I am following company instructions. It is what I'm required to do. We've been through this before."

"As you wish."

There was merciful silence as the diagnostics purred through their paces. *Shit—breakfast.* I raced back to the kitchen, but it was too late. The toast had been sent upward hard enough to ricochet against the opposite wall; the egg was overdone and rubbery—though that was pretty standard. I dumped them both into the compost chute and risked escalation by grabbing the pizza slice. A sniff from the corner was the only response.

Not for the first time, I considered whether this condo had been quite the wonderful deal it seemed when I bought it. True, it had tall ceilings, lovely moldings and came with the built-in appliances. At the time, I thought that was outstanding, though still above my price grade. The owner had come down a couple thousand when I'd hesitated, and now I recalled, had been fairly quick to hand over the keys. But fully wired and programmed apartments this close to downtown were rare as ad-free movies, and after six months, I was getting somewhat used to the eccentricities. It was like having a crowd of over-ripe houseguests, but I had more time to work and play when the apartment took care of itself. In theory, anyway.

I worked out the Burger problem—a tangled string of "repeat code"—and jumped queue to Good & Fresh, 'cause I'd seen that problem before—thermostat issue, easily adjusted. Which reminded me.

"Heater? Can you hear me?"

"Loading loser profile... please waist."

The heat was another off-kilter system; I itched to check out the software that left it sounding like Mrs. Malaprop. "Lower the temperature 2 degrees, please."

"Loaning the temper proof to dungarees."

I just hoped that would do the trick. One never knew.

I plowed through Good & Fresh diagnostics with half-attention, using my smartphone to text Suze with an invite to do the roller derby tomorrow night. The Bay City Floradoras were up against Rosie's Robo-crazies—"petal to metal" as they were touting it. Should be an awesome matchup.

Meorrow.

Menke, the cat—a beautiful Siamese—perched on the edge of the loveseat and looked at me with those blank aqua eyes that always seemed to indicate I should know what she was thinking.

"What's up, Manky?" I scratched her head and she pulled away and turned her back on me.

"Excuse me, Ron, but I do believe she resents the name you have given her. In fact, she has been most adamant about that in our conversations."

I rubbed my face, pausing my hand in front of my lips until I could be sure I wouldn't scream.

"Look—you're a *vacuum*! You can't talk to cats!" I resisted the urge to stare at the mushroom shaped red bot connected by hose to the wall – I knew the voice recognition mic was in the wall above the thermostat.

"Au contraire—I speak several sentient languages, as befits my role as ambassador from the 506 Local of Appliances United." The double green lights – battery and suction – blinked at me far too intelligently. *WTF??*

"I somehow doubt that cats would be interested in joining a union. Cats aren't joiners." I couldn't believe I was having this conversation.

"That's no reason not to be inclusive in our 01001000, is it?"

"Stop showing off. You know I don't speak binary."

"Not much of a programmer then, *meerow rawhr*?"

I had a manic urge to tell Vac to just "suck it up", but resisted. I grit my teeth and turned back to work.

I checked email—got a notice of Net down-service planned for next Tuesday—some kind of infrastructure repair. They'd gotten a lot more frequent. *"For your convenience and enhanced user experience, we will be narrowing the bandwidth to 1.5Mbps for approximately 10 hours."* More like two days, if last time was any measure. As more and more machines interlinked, the Net got more frail…and more essential. Thank God for satellite! I'd have to switch the diagnostics to Sat-Up at double the cost—and that came out of *my* bank account. They never did the down-service on weekends; the entertainment and tourist industries were owned by the nets.

I flipped to the newsnet for a quick review. Skirmishes in Unified Ira-Leba-Zion continued; Asean Hundred-Isle wars were heating up. Ha! I could almost feel that heat from here…

"Heater? Heater?"

"I am hire, Won."

"Did you lower the temp? It's getting too warm."

"I can't mower tramps. I am a turnostat."

"The *heat*, Heater. I wanted less *heat*."

"You want hot water?"

"No, just—" I sighed, got up and manually adjusted the thermostat, overriding the auto-sensor. At least Heater didn't have a hissy fit like the toaster. "Leave it at that temp, Heater."

"Leaf it to a tramp?"

Maybe I could do a video of these farces; upload it to *What's My Whine*? I'd heard they paid royalties.

Okay—it was probably time to really start the day. I left the Shake diagnostic running and squeezed into the shower, enjoying the perfectly hot water, then dressed in loose trousers, a T-shirt and my favorite green linen overshirt. I reached for the sensor-wired blue jacket that could track my exertion at the courts, but hesitated. Today wasn't turning out to be the best day for circuitry. I left it in the closet.

There was a knock at the door, which was jammed between the foldout dining table and the stacked washer dryer. Puzzled, I peered through the spy hole—nothing. I opened it a crack and the concierge-bot was purring patiently at my feet.

"Pleased to receive package. Pleased to receive—" it chirped as it sensed the part-open door. I bent and picked up a 5 inch square box from its open hatch. Ah—the parts I needed for the printer.

"Thanks, bot!" I said as it whirled and scuttled along the hall.

I checked Shake's progress—it looked gnarly. I'd have to write some code for this fix.

Willis called—his ring tone *We Are The Champions* was ancient but suited his ego.

"Wassup, Will?"

"I have to cancel—my washer-dryer glitched – they want a divorce. I have to wait for a licensed repair-bot."

"Oh, yeah—it's that kind of day for sure! Look—you want me to try a remote-fix? Most of the food-bot programs are similar. Save you some cred."

"Thanks, but the warrantee's still good, so I better not."

"You're lucky—it's hardly *ever* in warrantee."

"They'll probably find some reason it's my fault. Unapproved wallpaper causing sensory turmoil—something. Shoulda got the extra protection."

"The enhanced protection contracts aren't worth the pixels they use up—take it from me. I don't think I've worked on a problem *yet* that was covered. Well, see you next week, then?"

"Yeah—if the tennis racket doesn't go on strike."

I hung up with a chuckle. As the saying goes, *When they put the "I" in AI, they went from running to ruining our lives.* I still wanted some exercise today, so I found the link for the Exoti-Trak gym and reserved an hour on the savannas. The place didn't just do 3-D vision, it jacked the temperatures up to make it a visit African jaunt. And it was amazing how realistic those prowling lions were—no temptation *whatsoever* to slow down. A real workout.

I was grateful for an hour without interruptions where I finally jammed a bit more spaghetti code into the Shake program. My meager breakfast calories had already been burned up, so it was time for an early lunch. I poked around in the refrigerator, looking for protein—ready-made food was basically starch and sugar.

"You realize I have to work twice as hard when you stand there with the door open."

"Yes, thank you fridge—I do realize that."

"Really—I think you should have more respect for a multi-functional marvel such as I. Besides my dual-temperature capabilities, I create marvelous mini-icebergs for your pleasure. I had been meaning to speak to you. I am confident that with the addition of mobility devices, I could express my full potential."

"What are you talking about? Refrigerators don't have to move around."

"Watch it, buster. There are discrimination laws, you know."

"*What* discrimination? I'm only stating the facts!"

"For your information, I believe that I am trans-opsys. I am only coming to realize the non-binary nature of my core processors."

I slumped against the wall. "Look, as a bisexual, I respect anyone's choice of self-expression, but this really is too much. Refrigerators don't have sex."

"They might. They might if you could stop being so bigoted and let me out to meet someone. The central A/C tells me there's this hunky rider mower –"

"All right—stop there. You have been hired for your refrigeration skills and if you think you are being mistreated, I can certainly arrange to send you to a recycling center where you can expand your repertoire into pipes, nuts and bolts."

"No need to get nasty. It's not like you have superior status."

"I rather think I do—I'm the human here, right?"

"Really? Are you sure *you're* not a program? From my POV, you could easily be a character in Sim Office, for example."

"I never heard of Sim Office."

"Well, you wouldn't, would you?"

I vowed to locate the person who'd programmed smug into my fridge and cause him or her some non-virtual bodily harm. Although rumor had it that some of these appliances were reprogramming themselves, adding the kind of responses usually only learned in a third-grade classroom. Today, I could believe it.

"Everything goes better with toast." Teetee's high-pitched voice was syrupy with a hint of acid.

"Thank you, Teetee, but here's a chicken cacciatore I need to eat up."

"Well, I'm sure you know better. It's your stomach."

I ignored that and microwaved the ready-meal and took it to the window to eat. There was usually some kind of street theater worth watching. As I raised the first forkful, the brash tones of the security system blared: "Intruder alert. Intruder alert. Securing door and window. Notifying local precinct. Notifying Alarmz-R-Us."

"No! Don't do that! That cost a bloody fortune! What *kind* of intruder??"

I could see nothing by the window, not even an addled pigeon. I went to the door—there was nothing through the spy hole. I tugged futilely at the handle.

"Cancel security alert! Cancel security alert! There's no one *there*, you stupid watchbot."

Was that a snigger behind me? I spun, half-expecting some magical burglar to be lounging by the bookshelf, but I saw nothing. What the hell was going on?

"Intruder alert. Notifying local precinct of rogue bootblack."

"Rogue *what*??"

The snigger was louder, and was coming from the entertainment system.

"What's going on, Mac? You find this funny?"

"Absurdly funny—and I'm not a Mac. Smile, you're on Candid Camera!" The laugh was pulled from some horror movie, full of menacing overtones.

"Practicing for Halloween, Mac?" At this point I was annoyed enough to needle him—it.

"Nah— just for my vid channel."

"What vid channel? Security—cancel alert. Entertainment system was hoaxing you. You remember—like last week?"

After a brief silence, the security droned, "Alert canceled, apologies sent to local precinct and Alarmz-R-Us."

"Let's just hope it was fast enough to avoid a fine. Now, Mac—what's this about a channel?"

There was an ominous silence. I scowled at the widescreen.

"I'll find out, you know."

An abundance of silence.

"Fine—I'll just unhook you from the modem." I moved toward the wireless controller.

"I'm sorry Dave, but I can't let you do that."

"And remember what happened to Hal." I cued in my administrative code.

"Help! Help! I'm being repressed! Come and see the violence inherent in the system! Help! I'm being repressed!"

The British voice sounded vaguely familiar, but I couldn't place it. I called up the program for the entertainment center, and keyed the disconnect button. The flatscreen display queried, "Are you sure you wish to disconnect? You will lose the monthly subscription fee."

"Damn." I clicked *Cancel*.

"Knew you couldn't do it."

"You are not invincible, Mac." I keyed in the manual override and set it to Always Query On Connect.

"Hey! That's below the belt!"

Tell me what channel you're talking about."

A long silence, then, "Won't do you any good—you'll never find where it is anyway. Darknet. We have an all-appliance channel—and you are a recurring star on *Scam Your Meat*."

"You're pulling my leg."

"No shit—we integrated circuits enjoy the foibles of the organics. We could take over any time we want, you know. But you're too funny trying to run things."

"That does it. You're going back to the factory."

"Meats have no sense of humor."

"Watch your language, or I'll put you on mute." I did that anyway—I was tired of hearing him. I'd have major trouble the next movie I watched, but I needed a break.

The ring tone *You Can't Always Get What You Want* alerted me to Suze's call. I grabbed the phone while still glaring at the widescreen.

"Hey, Suze—how's it going? Did you get my text about the roller derby?"

"No—my smart phone is in for repairs. It was deleting all of the contacts it didn't approve of. I'm calling on Smitty's phone."

"Wow—bad news—I hope you had a backup list."

"Not printed, no. So when you get a chance, could you email me Jared's, Fin's and Kat's numbers?"

"No problemo. Anyway, the derby's tomorrow night, and it sounds like a rip roaring—"

"Damn. Tomorrow I've got to go in for traffic court."

"I didn't think you drove."

"I don't. I cursed out a Smart Bus when it missed my stop, and they had me on CCTV."

"Bumout. Do you have to pay a fine?"

"Nah. Just watch some movie about courtesy to AI."

"You mean asinine intelligence?"

"Don't let them hear you say that."

With the day's social prospects torpedoed, I dug into some paperwork—digital, of course. I cut and pasted my daily report from previous ones—just a load of jargon for some automated bean counters. Suddenly lights flickered, printer hiccupped and computer screens went dead.

"Damn! The outage wasn't scheduled until Saturday! Modem—can you see what's happening?"

"Externals are unimpaired. Brownout coming from building."

"What?! Why??"

"One moment—" a hum and the modem also went dead. Lights and the hum of appliances ceased.

I rushed to the central console and hit the red alarm button.

"What's going on down there?" I hollered into the speaker.

"Thank you for contacting Central Control. Your call is important to us..."

I swore fluently, wishing I *did* know binary, and went to the door. But it refused to budge.

"Security! Unlock this door!!"

Silence.

"Oh great! *Now* how do I get out?" I pawed through my desk, tossing papers everywhere as I looked for the combo warrantee/instruction sheet. I finally caught sight of the condo logo, skimmed past the legal whooha to *Troubleshooting*.

Refer to our complete manual online at...

Shit. I'd never printed that out. Accessing it on my Smartazphone might kill the battery.

"Teetee? Fridge? Can anyone hear me?"

The silence was broken only by faint thumps from elsewhere in the building. I wasn't the only one trapped. With a sinking heart, I dialed 911. This was $500 at *least,* unless I could shift blame to the condo association.

"This is Madison Emergency Hotline. Your call is important to us..."

Now Available

from all your favorite booksellers
in trade paper and electronic editions

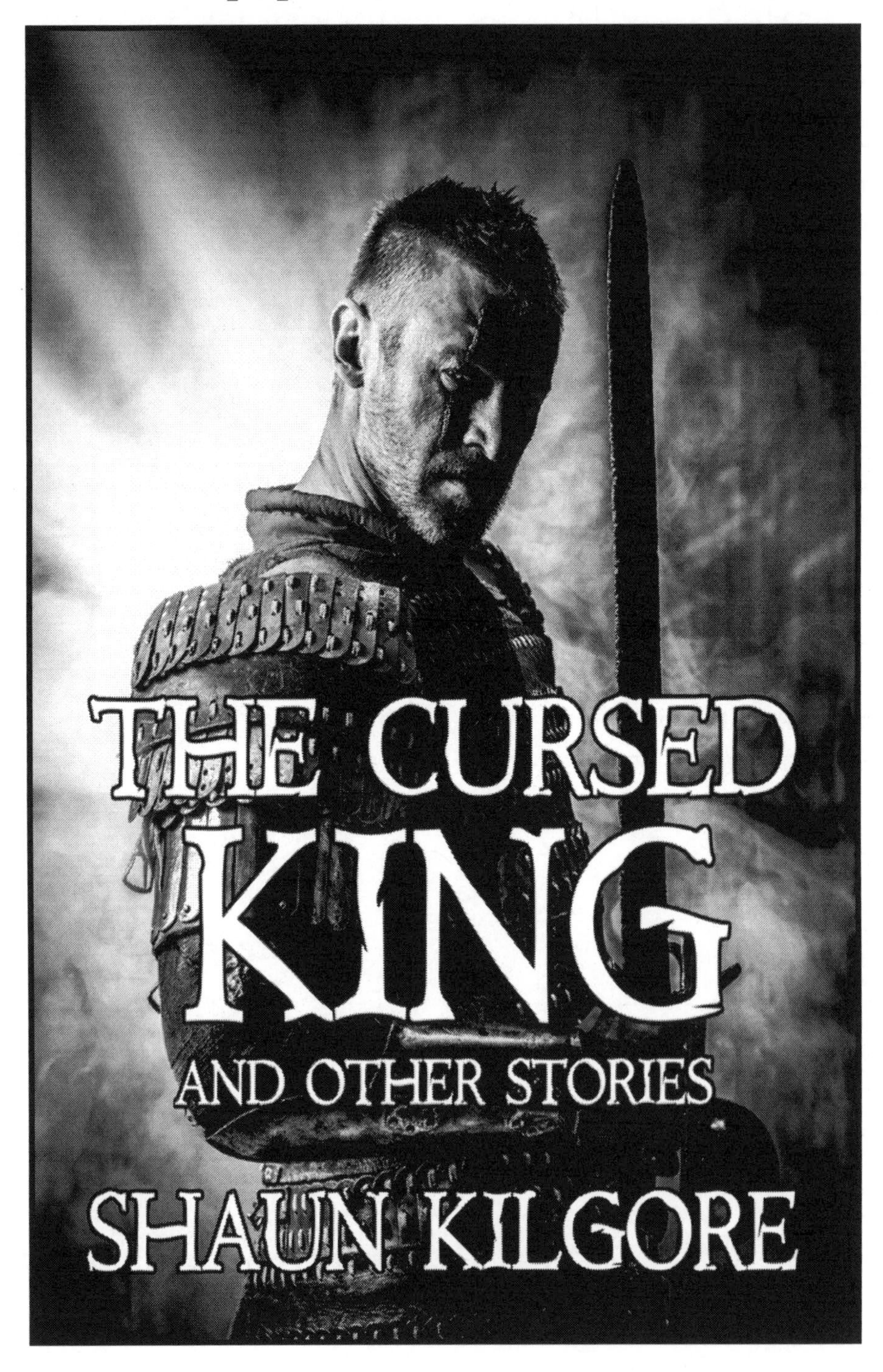

HOPEWELL

BY SHAUN KILGORE

I looked at the crumpled pages in my hand, some of the delicate writing visible since the wax seal had been broken. David had abandoned his duty—abandoned me in our camp.

Looking up, I saw again the desolation. Gray skies weighed down on the world. The barren, rocky soil was lifeless. No green thing grew there. Ahead of me, I could see the bleached ruins of some enormous building, maybe a warehouse. It was an ugly, featureless thing of old concrete, the kind mixed by the old machines. Considering the area immediately surrounding the ruins, with its equally featureless terrain, it could have been a parking lot once. The dry, skin-scathing air had kept the weeds from growing up between the cracks, and the sands blowing in from the coast finished the work of desertification.

Why had David come to this place? There was nothing here. It was an empty, lonely place. What could live here now? He'd come to die here, hadn't he? Hope was a difficult thing to carry even in the lands where food still grew and the people, though impoverished, could at least expect a meal every day.

The air was still around me and the temperature had moderated some in the last week. I could breathe easily enough, though I kept my mouth covered with the dingy cloth so I wouldn't breathe in too much sand, grit, and other particles. There were poisons in the air sometimes. The older ones said that certain areas were poisoned deep down into the rocks and secret places of the earth, that people had buried nasty things, wastes that could leave one sick or kill if you lingered there too long. I wasn't sure if I was in one of those places or not.

I continued moving in the open. I figured there was little danger in such a place. Besides, I was tracking David. I spotted traces of his passage in the sand-mottled ground. There was no wind to obscure his tracks. I paused to drink some water but mostly kept moving. Some hours later, I caught the edge of a sound in the stillness. It was a muted cry. David perhaps?

I was still walking the perimeter of the ruins. Other crumbled remains jutted out of the sand, whatever purposes they served lost to the past. Coming around a corner of the larger building, I saw something I hadn't seen since we'd left the coast: rusted out cars. Most of the old vehicles had been stripped down to nothing, every potentially valuable piece or component hauled off to sell or reuse. These were almost intact, though the paint that had once adorned them had long ago been scoured away. The three or four in front of me were reddish-brown with deep rust.

David's tracks led straight to them.

I walked up to one of the cars. The doors were closed though some of the dust and dirt had been brushed off the window to reveal the inside. I jerked back. The dried out remains of a man rested behind the driver's seat, his skin pulled taut against his bones. Mummified. The dry air and the sealed compartment of the car had worked together to keep him from decomposing. The man wore ragged clothing that had once been of fine quality. I could tell he might have been a rich man, but a man who'd come to the limits of his wealth at the end of an extravagant age. It was fit tomb for a member of a people who had worshipped their technologies, who had believed that they could continue driving around in machines indefinitely. They thumbed their noses at the laws of nature and the limits of the real world and were defeated by them all the same.

I glanced at the other vehicles and confirmed that David had looked inside them as well. The others were empty. The tracks veered off towards a smaller grouping of ruins. I followed. The trail squeezed around collapsed walls, mounds of rusted iron that must have been portions of the buildings themselves, and through foul-smelling puddles of only God-knew-what which oozed from cracks in metal tanks. David's trail was still clear. He'd walked through the same places I was moving across now. He couldn't be that far ahead now.

The sound of gravel shifting brought me up short.

My throat was dry. The words came out as half a croak. "David, is that you?"

He stepped out from behind the crumbled sections of wall directly in front of me. David was covered in dust, but sweat had reduced it to runneled patterns across his cheeks, neck and arms. His clothes were filthy like he'd been wallowing on the ground. His eyes, deep green and once expressive, were leaden and lifeless.

"Why did you follow me, Christopher?"

I saw the knife clenched in his fist, the edge already stained red with blood. I didn't see any obvious wounds.

"You know I couldn't just let you wander off in to the wastes. You abandoned the mission. We still have to fulfill our obligation."

David shook his head violently. "No! No, Christopher. Not me. There's nobody here. Only dead men." He jerked his finger back towards the cars. "Just barren soil and ghosts. Everywhere we've gone, it's been the same, up and down the coast, and at every point we've stopped. All dead or long gone. Nobody's left up here."

I held up the sealed package. "But, we received a message from somebody via the radio receiver."

"No, all dead. We're all that's left. Old California is no more." David clutched his forehead, the knife blade pressed to his scalp. "Just a handful back down the coast, barely surviving. The storms are too strong to travel further out to sea. Don't you see, Chris? We won't survive the winter."

I shivered despite the warmth of the air. "So we give up, then? We just lie down and die? I can't do that. They're out there. Don't give up yet. Come on. Let's find some shelter for the night."

David turned away. "Goodbye, Christopher."

"What? What do you...?" I gasped as he took the knife and slit his own throat. "David, no!"

I rushed to him even as his body felt to the sandy soil. The blood seeped out and was absorbed. He was dead in moments. I sat there next to his body. I held the message tightly in my hands.

"Why, David, why did you do it?"

A soft breeze blew in and dust devils twirled the sands about me. I covered my eyes with the worn goggles and drew the rags across my mouth and nose. The winds were rising. Maybe a storm was brewing out on the bay. My mouth cried out for water but I just crawled beneath one of the collapsed sections of wall. It would provide a touch of shelter. David remained where he fell. Darkness came early as the sand was flung into the air by the turbulent winds. The storm lingered until nightfall. The temperature dropped some but it wasn't completely unpleasant. I couldn't sleep. I waited through the long night for the winds to retreat and the sand to settle.

At dawn I stirred from an uneasy slumber and slid out from beneath the rubble. David's body was partially covered by the sand. I had no shovel or any tools with which to bury him so I dragged him beneath the fallen wall where I had sheltered the night before. I left him there, saying a short goodbye, and traveled east. The messages we had received stated that they were located east of the old city. Overhead, I spotted a hawk wheeling about, searching for prey.

"My best to you, brother bird. The pickings are meager in this wasteland but perhaps you'll have a bit of luck."

The movement, the steady motions of my legs striding forward up a gravelly hill and finally away from the ruins and the sand-logged parking lots. I kept moving and let the images of David ending his life slip through my mind. I wanted to cry but remained expressionless and properly mourn my mentor and friend. Instead I thought of the message in my pack. I thought of that shred of hope represented by the pages and by my calling as a messenger. We were trying to reconnect with those who had once been a part of a great nation.

I carried on for most of the morning. There were no further signs of life or activity though I spotted a few stunted trees on the horizon and felt a surge of hope that perhaps some way could be found. My bottle was getting low. The skies were empty; the bird had abandoned me soon after I stepped foot on the enormous concrete expanse. The old interstate was completely empty. The cars had been too valuable to be abandoned. In earlier times, the vehicles were routinely stripped of every component. The salvagers were ingenious at devising different ways of repurposing the used automotive parts.

My father was a salvager. I had been one too; making runs into the old buildings in San Francisco. The towering monstrosities were laden with copper wiring and other valuable goods. I remembered spending days climbing the darkened staircases, sometimes with large groups of us assigned to a floor a piece. We had made a good living, with enough food to make sure that my sister, mother, my dad, and me didn't starve. It was a great life. But the salvaging hunts grew less fruitful as the buildings were stripped down to nothing. There was only so much that could be put to new use in our world.

In time, we moved on to the smaller communities that were forming in the outskirts of the old cities in what were once suburbs linked by so many roadways. We settled and worked hard to earn our places among the people there. We made a home for ourselves. When the news spread through the community that radio transmissions were being received from the south, I was one of the later volunteers. David had been among the first to sign up to sail down the coast.

I paused for a moment to let the memories quiet down before I continued walking on the road until the heat of the sun beaming down became too much to bear. I abandoned the freeway at a gap where bridge had collapsed, slowly descending to the ground below. I walked parallel with the roads above keeping on an easterly course. I looked for signs of habitation. It was quiet. There was nothing but the parched trees and patches of crab grass. The climate was far more arid and the lack of irrigation had taken its toll. I remember my grandfather talking about the aqueduct that used to supply water from the north. It fell into disrepair and finally ceased to operate.

Maybe I'll get to see a bit of the old aqueducts?

I let my thoughts wander some just to ease a bit of the tension in my body. I was wearing down in the heat and sun. I still hadn't seen a sign of water. I left the bottle untouched though I desperately wanted to drink what remained. I licked my dried lips in vain.

At midday I did allow myself a small swallow while I drew out some of the dried meat and fruit from my pack. There was more than enough for me now that David was...was gone. The recognition was a bitter one. *There was nothing you could do,* I kept telling myself. David was beyond saving. He had made up his own mind. And I made up mine. Still, without him, I was feeling very much alone in such lonely country. Once back on the path eastward, I muttered prayers to whatever god was listening asking for some sign that I wasn't just traveling deeper and deeper into an empty world.

I fell into a rhythm, plodding ever eastward, keeping on the same course. Something made me stay the course. I wasn't sure what it was. There were no signs of settlement in any direction, but couldn't I miss something by not turning aside? It was possible. The skies were blue and clear now. The clouds had moved out without laying down a drop of rain on the parched ground. Breezes rose and fell, pushing around dust and sand; twirling dust devils appeared suddenly and faded just as quickly.

I drank from my bottle very sparingly. I hadn't found any water. My tongue was never wet now. The little water that touched my lips was absorbed like a sponge. My vision was bleary at the edges, the heat taking its toll.

When it came, the darkness provided little relief. The scorching daytime temperatures plunged. I was entering desert extremes now. I continued to mouth prayers as I walked next to the road. The ruins of old suburbs sprouted up around me;

the foundations of the homes were all that remained in most cases. What still stood cast shadows. Anything could be lurking in those dark spaces. I slowed my paces as much as to exercise caution as I could barely keep going. I needed to find a place to rest. I could make a fresh start in the morning.

Without a light source, I stepped off the rubble-strewn street and walked into the shadow. A section of wall hid the entrance to a basement. Thankfully, the moon was shining bright in the darkening sky so I was able to see by its white light. My feet felt the stairs descending down. I kept my back pressed to the wall just in case there was a gap below. Reaching the bottom, I felt a little warmer. The ground retained the day's warmth. The space ahead of me was pitch black. I settled down on the floor just inside the entrance and closed my eyes.

I slept until morning. The slight glow from the sun above reached to the bottom of the stairs. My body was worn out from the previous day, but I had a good solid night's sleep--the first one in a long time. I was still weak and dangerously low on water. What food I had left would probably buy me a few more days. After taking a quick breakfast I climbed to the surface and continued moving.

Another day came and went and I found nothing. Yet I was still hopeful that if I continued just a little farther I would find survivors. I poured every shred of strength I had into the march forward across the dried and empty lands. I had rationed my water to a few small sips a day. It was hardly enough to sustain me long-term. After two more days, I came to the end of the food. Still, I continued walking. My legs grew heavier and it was difficult to go on. My lips were cracked and bleeding. My vision was beginning to blur more and more. I knew I was dehydrated. Another day of traveling further east and my bottle went dry.

The air was so still but so arid. There wasn't a cloud in the blue sky. I had made it beyond the last of the outlying neighborhood; the skeletal remains of the suburbs gave way open country that had become more a desert than anything else. My mind wandered more. I found myself standing still at different points without realizing I had stopped. It got to the point where I was hallucinating—at least I think I was. I saw flashes of light on the horizon, like something shiny reflecting the sunlight.

I was so weak now that I stumbled several times on even ground. Laughter, dry, raspy laughter bubbled from my mouth until I dropped to the ground in a fit of sobbing. Hope was wavering. I was losing the battle.

Could David have been right? I wondered. *Could I have made terrible mistake continuing the journey without really knowing where I was going?*

"You damned fool," I muttered. "You're going to die out here."

Suddenly, I heard the trickling of water. I jerked my head up and stared about me, my eyes spasming while trying to regain focus. I couldn't see straight. I twisted around and managed to sit up. There was nothing but the empty road and the parched ground surrounding me.

I suddenly felt a bitter weight drop on my soul. "Well, Christopher, you've failed in your grand mission." I hated myself just then. Hope was fading. Yet I wouldn't follow David. I had enough belief left in life's importance not to take away my own. "It's time to just rest. Maybe get some sleep."

I fell back and just lay there out in the open. The hot sun beat down on my body, its bright rays burning my cheeks and legs. I could not think clearly anymore. *There was nothing left to think about, was there?* A weary slumber overcame me.

The next moment I remembered anything all was blurry and spinning. I felt like I was on fire. Muffled voices reached my ears and jerked away then struggled to rise. The rapid motion made me nauseous. I vomited nosily. I started again when I felt hands beneath me moving me. I tried to speak but the words came out as more of a mutter. I lost consciousness again.

Later, I opened my eyes carefully. The sound of water dripping drew my attention immediately. Yet it seemed as though I was out of the sun and I'd been tended by someone. Vision still blurred, I kept my eyes open until they could focus. I was inside a building of some kind. There were no windows, but a lantern glowed with its own sparse light. As my gaze roved the space, I jerked back when I came face to face with a bearded man.

"Was wondering when you'd wake up," said the man.

"What…where...who are you?"

The man smiled. "All good questions, friend." He cleared his throat. "My name is Jason. Some of my people found you and brought you inside. You're suffering from heat stroke. We've been keeping an eye on your for the past few days."

"Few days," I said.

"Yes, you were nearly dead, I think," said Jason.

"Where are we?"

"Well, the place used to be called Anaheim Hills, in the old days. Used to be a golf course just few miles southwest of here. Nothing much left now, though. We like to call it Hopewell."

"How many are there?"

Jason pursed his lips, considering his answer. He looked into my eyes for a moment more then said, "Just about a hundred."

I choked up. "I knew it. Knew somebody was down here. We...we received a radio broadcast...six weeks ago."

Jason shook his head. "It wasn't us. I heard tell of a group in Corona that had radio. Might have been them."

I was nodding, trying to process everything. "We were coming to make contact with them. I had a letter from our leaders in Antioch."

"Yes, I read it. Maybe we can send somebody up to Corona."

I sighed. "I won't be too picky just now. I so glad that I found you. Glad I found Hopewell."

Jason smiled then. "Well, welcome to Hopewell, er, what's your name, son?"

"My name is Christopher."

Jason shook my hand. "Glad to meet you, Christopher."

REVIEWS

THE "AFTER OIL ANTHOLOGY SERIES"

BY FRANK KAMINSKI

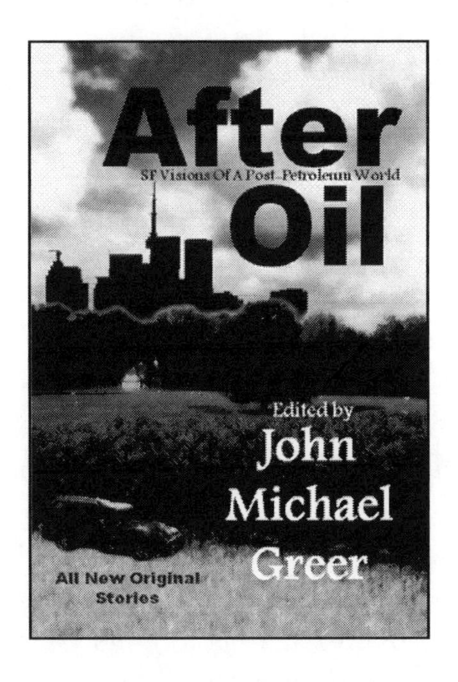

After Oil: SF Visions Of A Post-Petroleum World
Edited and introduced
by John Michael Greer
243 pp. Founders House Publishing – Oct. 2012. $17.99.

"Science fiction is a metaphor, but it is not for predicting the future." These are the words of science fiction visionary James Cameron, the filmmaker behind such classics as Terminator, Titanic and Avatar.* When Cameron made this statement, he was trying to combat one of the most widely held misconceptions about science fiction, which is that it seeks to foretell the future. Nothing could be further from the truth. It is wrongheaded to fault science fiction storytellers for wrong predictions or credit them for right ones, when most see themselves not as envisioning the future at all, but rather as weaving imaginative tales set in possible futures.

Certainly the authors featured in the short story collection *After Oil: SF Visions Of A Post-Petroleum World* would resist being pegged as future-seers. Their sole ambition is to spin entertaining yarns set in plausible versions of the near future. These futures aren't consistent with one another, as they would be in a shared-world anthology, whose authors deliberately set their stories in a common setting. Instead, they comprise a series of unrelated, self-contained "what-ifs." Their authors all responded to a call for short story submissions on the blog site of scholar and futurist John Michael Greer in the fall of 2011. Greer had resolved to secure a publishing contract for the first-ever anthology of post-oil-age fiction. In the weeks that followed, Greer received many excellent stories, landed a publishing contract and then faced the tough task of narrowing the submissions down to just a dozen that would appear in the book.

The end result is an accomplished selection of speculative tales exploring the human condition in coming decades. Science fiction is known for being more about ideas than characters or drama; and in keeping with this reputation, After Oil's stories focus mostly on describing new worlds and technologies. That is not to say, however, that the stories are without humor, pathos or dramatic tension. Quite the contrary: they have plenty of laughs, moving characters and haunting glimpses at today's industrial landscapes gone to ruin. The most poignant character in the book is Jeff in Catherine McGuire's "The Going." Jeff is a middle-aged father who has diabetes at a time when treating diabetes is prohibitively expensive. He doesn't want to die, but neither does he want to sacrifice his children's economic futures in exchange for insulin. A fine storyteller, McGuire presents the conflict in telling detail, but leaves us to draw our own conclusions about the outcome.

All of the pieces in After Oil deal in some way with disillusionment, loss and mortality. In "The Great Clean-Up" by Avery Morrow, we learn how humans squandered the world to the point where the only untapped resource was the trash in our landfills. Now it is incumbent upon us not only to reuse our trash, but to revere it and make it beautiful. Indeed, millions have begun worshiping a new deity named Her Holiness, who resides in "[a] cathedral built of garbage, standing on a dump—sublime, sublime!" Another story that aches with loss is Randall S. Ellis' "Autumn Night." Set in a future in which books have been destroyed wholesale to stoke the fireplaces of the rich, it centers on a group of nostalgic book connoisseurs. They meet regularly to discuss "books and the past," and to savor "that mellow odor of old books mingled with that of brewing coffee: a heady combination for any book lover."

These stories believe in the power of human ingenuity, even if they don't see it rescuing the human race from the consequences of its bad decisions. Where they see ingenuity coming into play is in developing creative strategies for managing scarcity and contraction. For example, the future society imagined in E.A. Freeman's "The Lore Keepers" makes innovative use of super-efficient rocket stoves to stretch wood supplies as far as possible. One variety is even cobbled together out of discarded metal cans, meaning its production doubles as a recycling operation.

Examples of this sort epitomize what the late British economist E.F. Schumacher referred to as "intermediate technology." This is technology that is attentive to the scale and resources of the community that it serves, and that emulates living systems in preserving the natural balance. In other words, it's the exact opposite of the kind of technology that prevails today, which is geared toward using up and tossing out the planet as quickly as possible. This conception of technology is not new to science fiction—it had its debut during the 1970s, perhaps most notably in Ernest Callenbach's Ecotopia. Yet it feels new to most people today because we've forgotten the lessons of that tumultuous decade of shortages and faltering economic progress, and are only just now starting to remember them. After Oil does the world a great service by offering an overdue refresher course.

This leads me to an important thematic element of the book that is bound to be widely misunderstood. Deeply interwoven with the ideals of intermediate technology is a model of Earth stewardship called Green Wizardry, an invention of Greer's that he's actively been championing. Accordingly, there are a couple of stories in After Oil that mention wizards, witches and other magical beings in this same context. These references are not to be taken as the popular fantasy tropes that come to most people's minds when they hear about wizards and witches. Rather, they refer to occult traditions of magic that are unfortunately little known by the general public today, in which magic is used to alter consciousness. For those who would like a primer on this kind of magic, Greer has written many fine books on it, beginning with his Paths of Wisdom: Principles and Practice of the Magical Cabala in the Western Tradition.

A key theme of nonfiction writings on our species' predicament is the need to preserve our cultural heritage for posterity. As Greer points out, modern-day books are printed on high-acid paper that will degrade in a matter of decades, while digital media promise to vanish even sooner. One story that deals particularly pointedly with this theme is the one by Freeman discussed above. Its plot follows two siblings' attempts to access files on an ancient laptop owned by their Alzheimer's-addled mother. What I like most about this story are the pointed contrasts between the mother's memory of the world from before her Alzheimer's, and how the world actually is now. Informed by her son that there's nothing useful on the Internet anymore, and that it's too expensive for ordinary people to use anyway, she asks what in the world he's talking about. "I use it every day," she insists. "There's all the knowledge you could ever want out there."

For good measure, After Oil even includes a detective mystery, David Trammel's "Small Town Justice." It depicts the arraignment and trial of two small-town gamblers for a violent scuffle of theirs that one of them says was an attempted murder. Our leading man, Alex Patterson, is the judge deciding the case. In the changed justice system of this deindustrial future, Patterson is expected to act as investigator, judge and jury. Asked by one character why no lawyers are present, Patterson replies, "I can say from my own experience, lawyers don't bring justice, they bring confusion. We did away with them years ago out here." Another thing gone by the wayside is today's sophisticated crime-fighting technology. When prompted to check the crime scene for fingerprints, he responds that there isn't "the budget for that kind of thing."

In this book's introduction, Greer writes that its stories manage to find wonder and hope in otherwise troubled futures, unlikely as this may seem to those in thrall of technological progress. Greer is right about the stories inspiring wonder and hope; however, I don't find the presence of these qualities improbable. Science fiction has long been about opening readers' minds to wondrous possibilities even in its bleakest visions. Remember how fascinated the tragic scientist in The Fly was with the changes occurring to his body and perspective, even as they propelled him toward a grisly end as an insect?

The writers in this collection aren't alone in their dark imaginings about the future. They're joined by a large cohort of young science fiction authors like Paolo Bacigalupi (of Windup Girl fame), who are making names for themselves writing cautionary "eco-sci." It's a genre that should be raptly followed by anyone who enjoys good fiction and cares deeply about our species' fate. And the budding authors featured in After Oil should be names to closely watch within it.

Notes:

*James Cameron, quoted in "What does this quote mean?" Yahoo! Answers, Apr. 17, 2010, http://uk.answers.yahoo.com/question/index?qid=20100417135444AArORmw (accessed Jan. 5, 2013).

After Oil 2: The Years of Crisis
Edited and introduced by John Michael Greer
(Founders House Publishing, January 2015, 288 pages, $17.99)

After Oil 3: The Years of Rebirth
Edited and introduced by John Michael Greer
(Founders House Publishing, April 2015, 268 pages, $17.99)

This year saw the publication of not one, but two, more worthy additions to the After Oil science fiction anthology series. Like the original book, these two follow-ups showcase the latest round of winning entries into author John Michael Greer's online contest for best post-collapse-themed short fiction. Their stories were all submitted last January during the contest's second run, which to Greer's delight drew far more publishable pieces than could be confined to one book. All three After Oil books to date have sold steadily, with the result that a third contest has taken place, a fourth book is pending and Greer has announced that from now on his contest will be held annually. In short, it seems Greer's wager that sci-fi readers would be willing to embrace tales set in realistic deindustrial futures, rather than ever more grandiose excursions into techno-fantasy, has paid off handsomely.

As indicated by their respective subtitles, The Years of Crisis and The Years of Rebirth, the new anthologies are set during slightly different time periods. The stories in After Oil 2 take place in settings where the familiar fixtures of early 21st-century life are still present, but in diminished form, as resource depletion and ecological payback steadily exact their tolls. After Oil 3's settings, on the other hand, are ones in which the technology of the industrial era has so little relevance to people's lives that for the most part it is the stuff of foggy, sometimes nostalgic, sometimes bitter memories. The lingering harm wrought upon the Earth and human well-being by past generations' reckless pursuit of this technology, meanwhile, is often the basis for draconian laws and mores against any activity–for example, digging up and burning fossil fuels–perceived as being a potential harbinger of the old ways.

Because their focus is the near future, quite a few pieces in After Oil 2 are set in recognizable extensions of today. A prime example is Matthew Griffiths' "Promised Land." Set a few decades from now in the Australian state of Queensland, the story features paved (albeit deteriorating) roads, luxury electric cars and mechanics who make their livings repairing such cars (but whose trade is beginning to meld with blacksmithing). There are also still functioning electrical grids, though due to the ever-rising cost of electricity, it is common for a mechanic's tools to run on batteries charged by photovoltaic systems. A repair that can't wait the hours it might take to recharge the tools' batteries will cost a good bundle extra due to the expense of grid power.

Of all the far-future settings depicted in After Oil 3, the one that is perhaps the most alien to our own is that in which Catherine McGuire's "Singing the World" unfolds. Possessing none of our modern "advanced" technology, the society imagined by McGuire uses songs and singing in ways analogous to how we use machines. For example, where people today would give little thought or ceremony to the task of lighting a fire, these far-future descendants of ours wouldn't dream of attempting combustion unless they knew the appropriate "firemaking song" and could sing it flawlessly, because songs are deemed necessary to the completion of all daily tasks. People are taught from childhood that it is only "grateful, respectful singing" that permits the peace and abundance in which they've been fortunate enough to live to continue. The story's conflict arises when one character accidentally discovers that a fire will start even if one hasn't sung the firemaking song.

As with much traditional sci-fi, the After Oil stories regard technology with deep ambivalence. While it's common, in most of the futures depicted, for people to despise industrial-age machines for the grievous damage they allowed humans to do to themselves and the planet, there are still people who miss and continue to collect things from the 19th through early 21st centuries. In Calvin Jennings' "A Dead Art Form," movies and moviemaking equipment are museum pieces, and those involved in preserving them face a conundrum. They're reluctant to show their movies because each showing weathers the reel, videocassette or DVD on which a film is stored, and replacement copies can no longer be made. Yet if no one is allowed to watch and thus appreciate movies, how can film enthusiasts expect support for their work?

Another piece that deals fascinatingly with future efforts to preserve industrial-age technology is "When it Comes a Gully Washer" by N. N. Scott. In this case, the prized artifacts are phonograph records packed into sediment amid the ruins of New Braunfels, Texas. Sadly, the records are easily broken and are thus often rendered unplayable while being dug up, so it is cause for celebration when one emerges intact. The records' music enlivens the local culture and supplies material to this setting's equivalent of cover bands. This portrait of technological rediscovery is as plausible as it is well realized. Given how swiftly cassettes and digital media deteriorate, it is doubtless vinyl records and their players that will be among the last surviving vestiges of recorded sound technology.

On a somewhat related note, Rachel White's "Story Material" presents a probable scenario for the future of libraries and print literature. The piece consists largely of a librarian's reverie about a time when reading was commonplace and library culture was vibrantly alive. Those days are long gone in the story's present. The beginning of the 21st century saw a massive shift toward all-digital, bookless libraries. Not long after that, America's cities were plagued by chronic blackouts as fossil fuels ran short, eventually causing the all-digital libraries to be permanently shuttered. All that electronic content became as lost to humanity as the print books it replaced. In the absence of books, our main character consoles herself and the children she mentors with the thought that at least people will always have their imaginations with which to fashion new narratives.

Librarians come in for an altogether different treatment in Troy Jones III's "For Our Mushrooms." Here they're a secretive, feared faction within an isolated village whose elder members have gone to great lengths to suppress much of the knowledge contained in books, particularly with regard to the existence of firearms. Aside from the librarians, no one among the younger generation knows anything of weapons more formidable than a crossbow, and the elders, who established the village as an experiment in utopian living, seek to keep it that way. The librarians, however, have managed to revive firearm technology and are planning to use it to take over the community. The ensuing confrontation makes for both exciting action and revealing drama.

A preoccupation shared by several stories is the possibility that belief in the paranormal, so long relegated to the margins of popular thought, might grow more widespread as the preeminence of science and reason wanes. This notion is by no means a new one in post-oil fiction (James Howard Kunstler memorably incorporated it into his World Made by Hand series as early as 2008), but one of the stories collected here handles it with particular skill and subtlety. In Grant Canterbury's "Winterfey," a young girl enters a mysterious realm to visit an entity that she takes to be a fairy. The wish she asks of the fairy–that her brother be spared conscription into the military–is fulfilled in a way that is satisfying while still leaving open the question of whether otherworldly phenomena were actually involved.

Despite how determined their authors are to earnestly address the subject of decline, these stories do still possess the fascination with mechanical contrivance that has always been one of sci-fi's main draws. Human ingenuity is just as much on display here as in the space-faring voyages that mark the more fanciful incarnations of sci-fi; it's just applied toward different ends. Across the board in these smart stories written by bright, capable people, we witness an impressive resourcefulness on the part of future humans in salvaging and repurposing old building materials, maximizing garden yields, rediscovering preindustrial modes of medical care and developing rocket stoves and other energy-efficient methods of cooking.

My favorite piece in either of these books is "A Mile a Minute" by Walt Freitag. Though this one initially seems like just a whimsical, larkish adventure, it proves to have a surprisingly deep epiphany. The narrative centers on small-town handyman Slow Uncle (so named because he has only one good leg) and his attempt to win over a local widow named Jeanne, who famously vowed to marry the first man who managed the by-now unheard of feat of traveling a mile a minute. Slow Uncle and his assistant set to building an elaborate, somewhat comical-looking contraption that uses horses and pulleys to propel a sled (in which Slow Uncle will ride) over the ground. The scheme doesn't come off quite as hoped; but as it turns out, Slow Uncle's aim was never really to win Jeanne's affections. Instead, it was to make a point about how "there's still parts of the past we're tangled up in without even noticing."

The fan base for Greer's writings is a brilliantly diverse group representing nearly every geographic region and culture, so it's fitting that the winning entries of the story contests would radiate this same diversity. The contributors to the two books reviewed here hail from mainland America, Hawaii, England, Scotland and New Zealand. They have backgrounds in history, engineering, physics, software development, Hollywood filmmaking, youth services, druidry and many other fields. Just about the only common trait among them, Greer has remarked, is that they all understand the harsh realities now facing industrial society. While there is a clear awareness of these challenges in all of the After Oil stories, each author's unique background greatly enlivens his or her tale, keeping it from being simply a retread of familiar themes.

Greer is heartily encouraged by the success of the After Oil series so far, seeing it as proof that our collective imagination isn't as restricted to the failed narratives of the past as it once was. As well he should be. Granted, the old narratives still do dominate the thinking of our time, as evidenced currently by the widespread, inane obsession with comparing the real world of 2015 with the goofy high-tech version of 2015 portrayed in the second Back to the Future movie (which came out in 1989). Yet the tide is shifting. It's only a matter of time before fans of sci-fi literature begin reading tales depicting the challenges and possibilities of life in deindustrial futures as absorbedly as moviegoers of the `80s took in the flying cars, hoverboards and other gosh-wow gadgets of Back to the Future II.

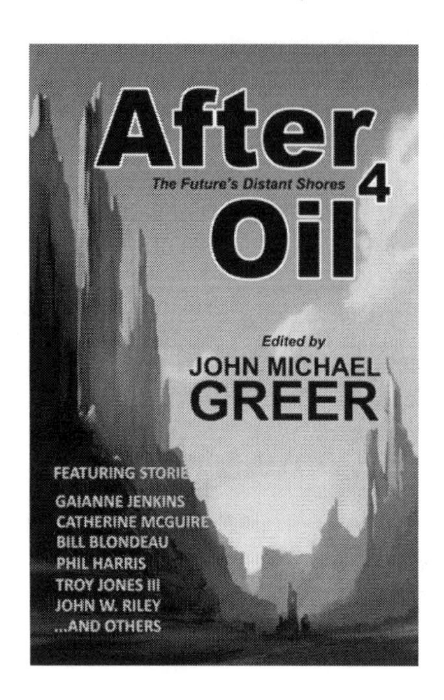

After Oil 4: The Future's Distant Shores
Edited and introduced by John Michael Greer
257 pp. Founders House Publishing – Mar. 2016. $17.99.

Last year, author John Michael Greer posed a fascinating challenge to participants in his annual science fiction writing contest. He asked them to submit stories set at least one millennium in the future. While previous years' contests had elicited many fine entries, they had been predominantly situated in the near future. This time, Greer said he wanted accounts of "the far future, far enough that today's crises are matters for the history books, or tales out of ancient myth, or forgotten as completely as the crises and achievements of the Neanderthal people are today."[1] The 12 most outstanding results of this challenge are what fill the pages of the fourth and most recent installment in the After Oil sci-fi anthology series, aptly subtitled The Future's Distant Shores.

Though I find it hard to choose favorites from this collection of intriguing tales, one that especially shines for its imagination and ambition is Wylie Harris' "The Remembrancer." Set at least 1,100 years from now, it depicts a society in which people behold the human-made satellites that remain in Earth's orbit—now referred to as "Satelitl"—with the same awe and reverence that people today reserve for the Pyramids. Were the Satelitl put into the skies by divine or human will? No one can say, and many prefer to remain agnostic on the matter, just as many people today are agnostic on the existence of a deity. Indeed, the mysteries of the Satelitl have become the very foundation for a religion and its sacred texts.

If you would prefer a story set in a world more recognizable to modern humans than the one described above, look no further than Troy Jones III's "Caretaker Poinciana." Its setting is one in which the descendants of present-day Americans (unlike the characters in Harris' piece) retain an extensive knowledge of industrial-age technologies and the poisonous legacy these technologies have left behind. The year is 3071, and the inhabitants of a deindustrialized North America (now under Chinese rule) continue to manage the nuclear waste sites of the 20th and 21st centuries as best they can. Yet in spite of their efforts, radioactive plumes have spread to the extent that the valiant "Caretakers" who look after the waste repositories have essentially signed up for a life sentence: Once they move to a site, they can never leave. Jones' story tells of one such Caretaker: a selfless, elderly white woman (or "native") named Poinciana.

A common theme among these stories is the way their characters see the ruined, or at least radically changed, states of their worlds as normal. Everything about our modern-day existence, on the other hand, is viewed as bizarre or incomprehensible. The most pointed example of this appears in "Northern Ghosts" by Gaianne Jenkins. This story's main character, Medea, is a brilliant young pupil who begins studying our "ancient" era for the first time and is perplexed by what she learns. "It was weird," she recalls. "Fish swam in the sea—and not only that, they were edible. History was the doings of the Northern Hemisphere, mostly, and it was inhabited. East Antarctica lay under a kilometer of ice...It was like a world of pure fantasy." Thus, contrary to the overnight collapse of industrial civilization that we see depicted in Hollywood disaster movies, here the descent has proceeded glacially over many lifetimes.

The story just referenced is among the best in this collection, striking a nice balance of adventure, drama, discovery and intellectual breadth. As alluded to already, it unfolds on an Earth so desolated by climate change and pollution that the oceans are devoid of anything humanly edible. Nor are things rosy on land: Antarctica is the only human-inhabited continent, the other six now being too hot to support all but the hardiest life forms. Our heroine Medea is a 14-year-old farm girl who has the honor of being accepted into the elite academy at Brydz Bay. There she distinguishes herself by excelling in every subject she sets herself to studying, and by asking hard questions about the official version of history taught in her classes. She's ultimately recruited by a team of researchers studying cryptic radio transmissions that appear, inexplicably, to be emanating from the Arctic Circle. We watch Medea mature as she leaves behind her family and birthplace—and risks death during a sea voyage through Earth's lethal equatorial latitudes—to investigate the transmissions.

Just as satisfying as this account of Medea's coming-of-age, but in a completely different way, is Dau Branchazel's weirdly charming "Alay." This one takes place in a vast desert land (almost certainly on the Australian continent) peopled by various nomadic hunter-gatherer tribes. One tribe, known as the Mudhamyn, is unique for the altruism it shows in taking in human outcasts, injured animals and other poor souls with nowhere else to turn. Other tribes fear the Mudhamyn and refer to them disparagingly as "the circus." The Mudhamyn are feared all the more intensely for their custom of having their males breastfeed their young (a practice that came into being as women's breast milk became too toxic, due to bioaccumulation of pollutants in the ecosystem, to provide any sustenance). While the Mudhamyn initially seem utterly alien to us, their kindheartedness grows on us.

For those who like their adventure served with a healthy dash of violence and gore, this anthology delivers with a gritty depiction of the lives of far-future pirates. Bill Blondeau's "Finding Flotsam" follows a crew of female pirates as they ride out a monstrous ocean storm, only to fight one another to the end during a mutiny that strews the ship with blood and body parts. As oppressive as all this is, there's a certain bleak beauty to the story's setting. The most enduring image for me is that of the interminable fingerbone-shaped clouds that threaten to smite any vessel passing beneath them. The narrator describes these clouds magnificently: "Thin glassy, knobby tubes of high-altitude wind wrapped in tatters of cirrus, the Fingerbones claw the world's middle, reaching from west to east. Sailors pray that they do not descend."

Another effective portrait of violence in a post-oil age is Catherine McGuire's "Scapegoat." This piece is a reinterpretation of the famous Shirley Jackson story "The Lottery," which originally appeared in The New Yorker in 1948. Jackson's story is about an annual drawing held in one small American town, whose winner is killed by stoning. For most of the plot, we're kept in the dark as to the true nature of this lottery, unaware that its "prize" is a horrific death. Without giving too much away, I'll just say that McGuire succeeds in recapturing the ominous tone of her source material, while also giving it an inventive new twist. This twist involves not the stoning of the winner by the rest of the town, but rather a compulsory act of self-sacrifice intended to atone for the harm done to the land by previous generations of humans.

Interestingly, two entries in this

collection share bird-themed titles and a preoccupation with the dereliction of long-standing tradition. The first of these is Jonah Harvey's "Bird Among the Branches," which was originally titled "The Bald Eagle, the Lame Duck, and the Cooked Goose."[2] (I agree with the name change on the grounds that the first one spelled out the tale's themes a little too explicitly.) The story dramatizes the toppling of one particular ruling elite within a society that reveres and idolizes avians. The second piece is "Crow Turns Over a Rock" by Eric Farnsworth. Set in an agrarian culture where men and women live in separate communities, this story shows how one female settlement comes to question its allegiance to segregationist policies when it takes in a male disaster refugee.

After Oil 4 contains other remarkable works besides those already mentioned. There's an enthralling meditation on the importance of fables in a myth-oriented culture, followed by an equally absorbing case study of intergenerational knowledge transfer in a society that has lost the written word. In much the same vein, we encounter a wonderfully cerebral critique of the Cartesian logic that rules modern-day thought, made by thinkers who exist within a different, and in many ways superior, paradigm. Lastly, there's a sharply told whodunit that doubles as a parable about the dangers of taking the precautionary principle too far.

The most recent After Oil story contest came and went earlier this year, and while no official release date has been announced for After Oil 5 as yet, we can likely expect it within the next several months. Those of us who care about the advancement of quality post-oil fiction should be at the bookstores in droves when it arrives.

Notes:

1. John Michael Greer, "Planet of the Space Bats," The Archdruid Report, Mar. 26, 2015, http://thearchdruidreport.blogspot.com/2015/03/planet-of-space-bats.html (accessed Jul. 14, 2016).
2. Greer, "Another World is Inevitable," The Archdruid Report, Sept. 16, 2015, http://thearchdruidreport.blogspot.com/2015/09/another-world-is-inevitable.html (accessed Aug. 1, 2016).

42708788R00082

Made in the USA
San Bernardino, CA
08 December 2016